Two Minutes for Roughing

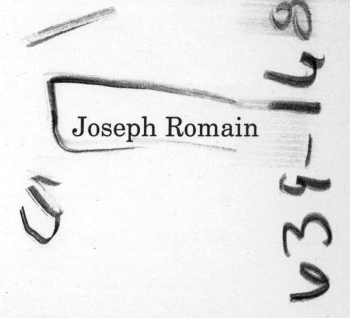

Joseph Romain

James Lorimer & Company, Publishers
Toronto, 1994

James Lorimer & Company Ltd. acknowledges with thanks the support of the Canada Council, the Ontario Arts Council and the Ontario Publishing Centre in the development of writing and publishing in Canada.

Cover illustration: Daniel Shelton

Canadian Cataloguing in Publication Data

Romain, Joseph
Two minutes for roughing

(Sports stories)
ISBN 1-55028-459-2 (bound) ISBN 1-55028-458-4 (pbk.)

I. Title. II. Series: Sports stories (Toronto, Ont.).

PS8585.053T8 1994 jC813'.54   C94-931906-6
PZ7.R65Tw 1994

James Lorimer & Company Ltd., Publishers
35 Britain Street
Toronto, Ontario M5A 1R7

Printed and bound in Canada

Contents

1

Mickey Tanaka

It all started with Mickey Tanaka. If it hadn't been for Mickey, I would have spent the whole season as an afternoon rink rat: a guy who hangs around the park, shovels the ice, and gets to play hockey when there aren't enough "real players" to make up teams. With Mickey, it was all different. It was fast and furious. It was my first year as a Metro Cat.

It was the year I learned a lot about my parents, and they learned a lot about me. In the spring they had separated, just after my twelfth birthday, and by Christmas, things were looking a lot different. It was also the year I learned to control my mouth. If it hadn't been for Mickey, I'd still be sounding off at people and paying the price. That winter, when the price for smart remarks went through the ceiling, I had to learn that it just wasn't worth it. Because of Mickey and the Metro Cats, I learned to control my temper.

It began on a cold Sunday morning. My mother picked me up at my dad's place on Saturday night. I was getting pretty tired of being shuffled back and forth between Dad's apartment downtown and the new house we were renting in the east end of Toronto. I don't know why they had to move so far away from each other. When I stayed at my dad's place, he'd bring me to school at eight o'clock. In the spring, it wouldn't be bad, but in the winter, it gets pretty cold hanging around the school yard waiting for the bell. Anyway, I only had to do that on Thursdays and Fridays. On Saturday night, my mom came to get me and I'd get to sleep in my own bed.

That first week of December, the city started flooding the rink in the park. They were flooding it on Saturday night when my mom and I drove past, but when I got there in the morning, it was covered by ten centimetres of fresh snow. I had my skates on and a light plastic snow shovel under my arm. Whizzing end to end with the snow shovel was fun, but it was still a lot of work to get all the white stuff off the ice.

I was about halfway done when a girl from my class came by. She didn't say anything, she just stood watching me zipping from end to end, pushing the snow along to the edge of the rink and packing it up against the edge of the ice. I figured that when they flooded the rink next time, there would be a hard crust around the edge and it would act as an end board.

I didn't really know Michelle Tanaka. I knew her name and I knew that she was smart in class, but that was all. I didn't really know many of the kids well. I'd only been at Sir Henry Pellatt Public School since we moved here in late October, and I hadn't made many friends. I had half the rink cleared when Michelle came over and spoke to me.

"Hey, you're doing a pretty good job. Can you use a stick as well as you move that shovel?" She had a sort of husky voice, like a boy's.

"Yeah, well, I'm not exactly Mario Lemieux," I said. I wondered if she knew who Mario Lemieux was. "You're Michelle, right?" I asked.

"Well, I'm not exactly Michelle Pfeiffer ..." she said. I wondered who Michelle Pfeiffer was. "My friends call me Mickey. What about you? Do you like being called Lester or Les?"

"Les. I hate Lester!" I was used to being teased about my name. Who would name a kid Lester Lewchuck?

"It'd be worse if you were called Michelle!" She was laughing. She had big teeth, like they were too big for the rest of her. She had short black hair, a small, sort of flat nose, and in her parka and big boots, she looked like an arctic explorer.

"I'm a goalie," she said, walking through the snow and stepping over the bank. "I'll help you clear if you want, and I'll bring my gear." She checked out the surface of the ice with her boot.

"Sure," I said, "but forget the shovel. I'll be done before you get back." I figured it was all right. She was a girl, but she seemed OK. Besides, a goalie is a goalie!

Mickey went home for her equipment, and I picked up the pace on the shoveling. I was nearly done when I heard them come up behind me.

"Hey," said a familiar voice. "Some turkey has done the hard work for us." It was Lenny Smith.

If you look up Neanderthal Man in the encyclopedia, you can see a picture of Lenny Smith. The Neanderthal Man has a large forehead and a very big mouth, but he has a very small brain. That's Lenny. Big and stupid. Everybody was afraid of him.

Roddy is Lenny's kid brother. He's more like Peking Man. He's not so ugly, and he's a little smarter. With his glasses, he almost looks intelligent. He's not exactly rocket scientist material — this is his second year in grade seven — but he's closer to human than ape.

I blew into my hands, traded the shovel for my hockey stick, and threw a puck out onto the ice. I could see them coming across the park laughing and throwing snowballs at each other. Their dog was snuffling around by the swings, doing his business. I circled the rink, pushing the puck along in front of me, trying not to lose it under my skates and look like a goof. The Smiths thought *everybody* was a goof, and I didn't want to give them any ammunition.

"Thanks, goof. We didn't even need the shovel!" Lenny said, sticking his shovel into the snowbank.

The third member of the Smith gang was Delgatto. He was probably smarter than either of the Smiths, but he hardly ever said anything, so you couldn't be sure. He just laughed all the time — squeaky and high pitched. His family were Catholics from somewhere in Africa. He probably had a first name, but nobody ever used it. He was just Delgatto. Maybe it meant something in some African language. He always wore a leather All Star jacket and kept his hands in the pockets.

"It's Lester Loser!" Roddy cackled. "Ya wanna play hockey, loser?" The three of them were skating in a circle around me.

"No, thanks." I tried to skate clear of them. I didn't want anything to do with these guys, but I didn't want to look like a wimp, either.

"Sure, you do," Roddy said, taking the puck. Roddy is in my class, but I never speak to him outside school. If he goes one way, I always make a point of going the other. He's not really big, but he sticks close to his brother and talks like he's tough.

"So the teams are us and you," he sneered, pushing the puck over to Delgatto. Delgatto had one hand in his pocket and his stick in the other hand. He didn't seem to have any trouble stickhandling that way. He skated toward me and slipped the puck between my skate blades over to Lenny.

"Yeah!" Lenny said, setting his blades firmly in front of me, flipping the puck quickly from side to side. I wasn't about to muscle the puck away from him. I glided toward him and he slipped it across to Roddy. I turned to go after Roddy, and he passed me the puck. "Here you go, loser," he jeered.

Great, I had the puck. Not great. Delgatto and Lenny Smith came slamming in from either side of me, and I went sprawling down to the ice.

When I sat up, they were skating in circles around me, slapping the puck across the ice, coming closer to my head than I thought was funny. "Why don't you guys buzz off!" I said.

"Hey!" I heard Mickey call from across the park. "What are you jerks doing!" I watched her waddle through the snow with her pads on her legs, waving her stick over her head. She looked like a giant penguin protecting her nest. "Get lost, Smith!"

"If it ain't Miss Puckstopper, the Great Girl Goalie," Lenny sneered at Delgatto. "We could use a target, eh?"

"OK, we can use Lester the Loser as the puck," Roddy added.

I stood up and got my shovel. I didn't need this. Guys like the Smiths are the reason I've never played much sports. It always seems that the meanest and the loudest guys get the best of things. I'd rather do homework than waste my time on these weeds.

"So where are *you* going?" Mickey called over to me.

I didn't have a smart answer for her. I shrugged.

"He's goin' home to play some checkers. He looks like he's ready for milk and cookies to me. All this hard work, ya know," Lenny said.

"Give him a nickel for all his hard work, Delgatto," Roddy smirked. Delgatto flipped a coin onto the rink.

I didn't know whether it was a nickel, a quarter or a dime, but I kicked it across the ice. "I hope you break your leg on it, Smith," I said.

Delgatto laughed at me. I guess he figured the Smiths would come over and punch me out and he thought that would be funny. But they didn't. Lenny flipped my puck out toward the swings where his dog was sniffing. He suggested that I could take the puck and do some uncomfortable things with it.

"Hey, Les," Mickey glided across the ice toward me. "You going to play checkers all by yourself or can I come along?"

"Sure," I said, without even thinking about it. I forgot she was a girl. Since I was about six or seven, I hadn't had a friend who was a girl. At school, there were girls who you'd play with at recess, but you wouldn't have them to your house. They were girls.

But I didn't think about it just then. I needed a friend, and I liked Mickey. So we went back to my house to play checkers and drink hot chocolate.

I wasn't sure how I was supposed to act, having a girl come over. But Mickey wasn't any different from anybody else. We clacked along the sidewalk in our skateguards, and she told me what jerks the Smiths were, how they were on her hockey team and thought they were hot stuff. My house was only a block and a half from the park.

Mickey was into music. She liked Bryan Adams and Neil Young. "My dad went to school with Neil Young," I said. "He used to come to our old house for dinner and for parties." She flipped out when I told her that. She slung her helmet over the blade of her stick and laughed.

"Have you heard him play 'Harvest Moon,' like, *live*?"

"Sure," I said. I couldn't honestly remember if he had ever played that song at our house, but he probably had.

"Cool. Anyway, do you really want to play checkers? Like, my *grandfather* plays checkers. He always wants us to play with him."

"Yeah, sure. I haven't played checkers since I was a kid. My dad used to play with me. He's not living with us right now ..."

When Mickey and I came in the side door my mom was in the kitchen, listening to the radio and drinking coffee. She was pretty surprised when she saw us. She didn't *say* anything, but I could see her raise her eyebrows when Mickey took off her parka. It was obvious that Mickey wasn't one of the boys.

I introduced Mickey and we went into the dining room and I got out the game. When I went into the kitchen to microwave some milk and get some cookies, my mom said, "So who's your girlfriend?"

"She's not my girlfriend, Mom, she's a goalie!" I insisted, even though it sounded stupid. "We're going to play checkers until the ice is clear of human debris." I didn't explain about the Smiths and Delgatto. I figured she'd say something stupid like I should stand my ground, or I should make friends with them.

"You're going to play *checkers*?" she asked, as if she suspected we were up to something.

"Yeah, Mickey plays all the time with her grandfather."

"Oh, fine. Great. Checkers. What do I know? I didn't think checkers were cool ..."

"Gimme a break, eh?" I said, wagging my head and swinging the kitchen door open with my foot.

"What do you mean about *human debris*?" she called after me.

"Never mind!" I yelled back. "My mother is the nosiest person alive," I said to Mickey. "You want to be red or black?"

"Red," Mickey said without hesitation. "And she's not the nosiest person alive. *My* mother got the award last year when my sister started going out with boys. Now my mother wants to know *everything* that happens *every* day. 'Where are you going? How long will you be there? What's the phone number? Don't talk to strangers ...' *She* is the nosiest person on earth."

"I guess it's weird, being a girl, eh?" I said. I was embarrassed as soon as I said it. I mean, Mickey *was* a girl, but neither of us had mentioned it. Now I was calling her weird. I didn't mean *she* was weird, I only thought it was different. Maybe it was *normal* for her to hang around with boys, but for me it was a bit strange.

"Yeah, it's *weird* all right. And a drag. My brothers get to do anything they want, but if my sister, Suzie, or I want to do anything, we have to play twenty questions. I mean, I know it's different for girls, but it's not fair." Mickey took one of my checkers and was closing in on my front row.

"I wouldn't know," I admitted. "The only girl I know is my mother, and she doesn't really count. My dad didn't like her very much …"

"Divorced?" Mickey asked.

"No, separated. They split up this spring. I mostly live with her. She's all right. My dad's cool, too."

I moved my checker in for the kill. Next turn I would take it. "Your move," I snickered.

"I've got one of those television families," Mickey laughed. "Two boys, two girls, two parents, Sunday dinners, and all that. It's OK, but these days it seems kind of strange. I even *like* my family. But don't tell anybody," she whispered. "You're supposed to, like, think they're all creeps.

"Crown me." She had one of her red checkers in my last row. "Haven't you ever *played* checkers before?"

It was stupid. I just hadn't seen it. Mickey won that game and the next one, too. We were on our third game when she asked, out of the blue, "Why don't you try out for the Metro Cats?"

"You mean your hockey team?" I thought about it. "I can skate, and sort of push a puck around, but I've never played on an organized team … Besides, aren't the Smiths on the Metro Cats?"

"Yeah, so?" she said. "And so is Delgatto. They're pretty good players."

"Thanks for the invite, but it's probably a bad idea. I wouldn't make the team anyway."

"They have a tryout, but really all you need is the equipment and a hundred dollars. We've got four or five empty spots on the bench. You could join. I'll practise with you. I'm pretty good."

"Well, besides" — I was thinking fast, I wasn't sure I wanted to join a hockey team — "I don't have the gear. I've got a stick, a helmet and a couple of pucks, but I don't have pants, and shin guards, or any of that stuff …"

"No problem. I've got brothers. They're bigger than you, but that's good, 'cause they won't notice when I borrow their old stuff. So it's on." She didn't leave me much of an excuse. "Saturday morning you come to the practice. Between now and then, I'll make a hockey player out of you."

And that's how I met Mickey Tanaka, and how I changed from the invisible new kid to a rookie right winger for the Metro Cats Hockey Club.

2

My Life as a Jock

My hockey lessons started on Tuesday. Mickey showed up at my house with a big red equipment bag right after school. When I answered the door, she slung the bag onto the front porch and grinned.

"Here's everything you need, Les. Suit up!" She was wearing her goalie equipment, and looked about a hundred kilos heavier than she really was.

Mickey waddled in and flopped down on a chair in the kitchen while I dragged the bag into the house and up to my room. I could hear her and my mom talking while I pulled the stuff out of the equipment bag. I wasn't sure how to put some of it on. I was struggling with the shoulder pads when I heard the two of them start laughing. They were probably laughing at the idea of me trying to figure out all this gear. This stuff should come with an instruction book.

The worst was the jock. I pulled out this thing that looked like something my mother kept in her top drawer, and tried to imagine what it was doing in a bag of hockey equipment. I was just about to put my arms through it when all of a sudden I turned beet red and realized what it was. There was a little pocket in the front for the cup. I *wondered* what that hard plastic thing was for ...

Once I got the jockstrap figured out, and squirmed into socks and garters, the rest was a piece of cake. How could anybody *skate* much less play hockey wearing all this stuff?

Mickey and I headed across the road and down the street to the park. She was lugging the net. I carried my bucket full of pucks.

There was nobody on the ice when we got there. There were a couple of hopeless basketball addicts shooting hoops on a big hunk of pavement they had cleared, but there was nobody skating. I pulled on my helmet and took a few turns around the ice. It was good: hard and smooth.

Mickey was setting up her net about three metres out from the edge of the rink, and scraping up the ice in front with the edge of her skate blade. "What are you doing?" I asked her.

"Makes it slower," she called. "If the ice is roughed up a bit the puck slows down when it gets here."

I had seen goalies doing this on television, but I never knew why. A lot of what they do in sports looks like strange, ancient rituals. Baseball catchers spit, batters do a little shuffle before they step up, I just figured that goalies did a little dance in front of their nets.

"The first thing you have to do is warm up. If you don't start by stretching, you won't be able to do this tomorrow. You're gonna hurt so much you won't be able to get out of bed. You can do it this way or the hard way." She sounded like a gym teacher. She had me doing leg raises, sit ups, ham string stretches and pushups before we ever got to the shooting part. Mickey was amazing. She brought the pail of pucks and set them up in little piles around the ice, and I was commanded to skate from one to the other and shoot them at her. She looked like Darth Vader, shouting out orders and pushing away everything I was able to shoot at her. The Force was with her.

"Does anybody ever score on you?" I asked, puffing and chugging across the ice, letting a wrist shot fly, which missed the net by a metre.

"Not on their first day out," she hollered. "Don't look at the puck. Look at where you want it to go. Look at the spot and just push the puck at it."

We did this for two and a half hours. Sometimes Mickey would pass the puck out and I'd try to get it past her, or I'd make rushes up the ice and try to deke around her. I never scored. Not even once. From time to time Mickey would grunt something like, "nice shot" or "you got it!" but she always had the puck in her glove, or under her leg. There was no question about it: Mickey Tanaka was a superb athlete.

That's really all I remember about Tuesday, and Wednesday, too. Thursday I got off easy, because I had to go to my dad's place until Saturday, but Mickey made me practise until he came to get me around seven, and she gave me three hockey books to read before the tryout at the rink.

I figured that after three days of Mickey shouting and me shooting pails of pucks, I knew about hockey. So when my dad drove me to the Eastern Arena early Saturday morning and dropped me off in front of the rink, I figured I was ready for the Metro Cats.

I was wrong.

Playing hockey on your own ice rink, or one in a park, with a girl goalie telling you what to do is one thing. But getting dressed with a bunch of twelve-year-old boys and playing hockey full out for an hour is another thing completely.

I knew a lot of the faces in the dressing room, and a few names, but nobody was very friendly. They all just put on their equipment and talked to each other. The kid closest to me was Ty Pulleyblank. His father and my father were friends when they were married to our mothers.

I recognized him right away, from the pictures at our house, but he didn't seem to know me. I thought I'd observe for a while. Not say anything. Ty was round. He was fat, but he was big, too, like one day he was going to grow into all that fat, and he wouldn't be fat any more, he'd just be a huge guy.

The coach came in and stood by the door with his arms folded. He had the sleeves of his red and blue jogging suit rolled up. He looked wiry and tough. He drummed his fingers against the door beside him. "Come on, men," he called. "Let's not take all day! I want your butts out on the ice in three minutes!" Then he sauntered out of the room.

Everyone shut up when the coach came in. When he left, they started talking and laughing.

As I skated out through the gate, the coach called to me.

"You're the new kid?"

"Yeah," I said, skating over.

"Yes, *sir*," he said. "You say 'yes, sir,' or 'yes, Coach,' or 'yes, Mr. Coleman,' but you save your lip for your line mate." At first I thought he was kidding, but something about his expression told me that he wasn't. "You're defence. Play on the red team. Paid your money?"

I thought I was going to have a tryout. I just stood there and said, "Yes, sir."

"Good. I'll have your jersey next week. You're number 16. Let's see you play hockey."

That was it. He didn't even ask my name. This wasn't looking good. Then Mickey came out from the other end of the rink. She didn't have her pads on, and she had a regular stick. Another kid, Rollie, was dressed for the net. Mickey was stretching and going through her warm-up routine.

"Get a load of her," Coach Coleman said. He was watching Mickey with his eyes narrowed, like he didn't like what he saw. Then he snorted and sucked at a plastic coffee cup.

Mickey was the best kid on the ice. By far. Nobody else was much better than me. They just paid a hundred dollars and bought the equipment. Some of the guys obviously had played a lot, but nobody really stood out except Mickey.

About five minutes into the practice, a guy with red hair skated out onto the ice. Mickey whipped the puck across to him and shouted his name. "Glen!" she called. "How's it goin'?" He snapped up the pass and cradled the puck on his stick and fired it into the empty net. Before he had a chance to answer, the coach called him over to the bench.

"Macklem!" Mr. Coleman yelled. "How come you're late again?" Glen sailed over to the bench and pulled his helmet off.

"I had to take my sister to her dance class ..." he began.

"I don't want stupid excuses. I want my men to arrive on time! This is a *team*. This is the Metro Cats. We show up *on time* and ready to work. If this team is going to win the division, it won't be after your sister's dance classes are over! Show a little respect for the team and get here on time, or you'll find yourself spending a lot of time on the bench! Do five laps and get busy with it."

Glen pulled his helmet on and mumbled to himself, dashing back and forth across the length of the rink while Coach Coleman stood watching him.

The practice was half over when the Smiths and Delgatto swung over the end boards. They were like rain at a picnic. We were having a good time. The team had been broken down into two scrimmage sides, one red and one blue. It didn't seem much like a practice, since all we were doing was playing a game, but it was great. Everybody was yelling and furiously rushing from end to end. Then the Smiths came on and everybody sort of stopped and skated around in circles.

Delgatto headed for the red team, and the Smiths took their places on the blue team. They were all forwards. The coach slid out in his boots and glared at Delgatto. Delgatto laughed.

"What are these people always laughing about?" Coach Coleman sputtered at Lenny Smith. He didn't wait for an answer. And he didn't tell them they were late, either. He bent over and dropped the puck between Lenny Smith and Delgatto and shuffled out of the line of fire.

These guys were playing for keeps. Lenny won the draw and passed the puck to Roddy, knocking one of the smaller kids down on the way.

Roddy tried to get past Ty Pulleyblank, but Ty lifted his stick, took the puck from him and made a rink-wide pass toward Mickey. Delgatto flew in from nowhere and snapped up the pass before it got to Mickey. He charged across the blueline and stick-handled his way around the blue team's defence. The Smiths were all over Delgatto, poking and shoving everybody in sight. That was how the practice went: kids were getting knocked around the ice as the Smiths and Delgatto battled it out to score on each other's teams. It was not exactly what I call fun.

Every time the puck came near me, it was followed closely by a flying Smith, who would crash into me and skate away with it. Nobody tried too hard to keep the puck away from them. Mostly, we were all trying to keep from getting hurt. Everybody except Mickey, of course.

When she got the puck, she and Delgatto would cruise up the ice flipping it back and forth, keeping it away from the Smiths until one of them hooked, tripped, slashed or charged in to take it. The coach called no penalties. He had nothing to

say at all. Finally, it was over, and we all clacked off to the
dressing room.

There were no parents in the dressing room. Coach Coleman had a rule: the dressing room was for the team. "If your
mummy wants to watch, she can watch from the stands. If she
wants to wait for you after practice, she can wait in the lobby.
The dressing room is for me and my men." When we left the
rink, Coach Coleman was still sitting on the bench, writing
something on his clip board. Then he barged in moments later
and gave us all a tongue lashing. "You look like a bunch of
wimps," he said. "The best one of you is the girl. You bunch
of woosies ought to be ashamed of yourselves."

Roddy Smith stood behind Coach Coleman mimicking
him. Delgatto stood there with his hands in his jacket pockets,
laughing like a hyena. "What are *you* laughing at, Delgatto?
Why are you people always grinning like monkeys?" he
asked. His nose was red, and he could have used a shave.

Delgatto just laughed, and Mr. Coleman stomped out of
the dressing room. "Game next Saturday," he called over his
shoulder. "The North Toronto Tornadoes. Don't be late."

Delgatto laughed some more. Lenny Smith took Ty
Pulleyblank's thermos and drank all the hot chocolate.
"Thanks, turkey," he said.

And that was what I had practised for. To get knocked
around by Smiths and glared at by the coach. That was the
Metro Cats.

3

Lost in Space

My life was getting more complicated. When I arrived at school now, I wasn't just the new kid, I was now Mickey's friend. And I was a Metro Cat. Some of the other kids on the team, the ones who ignored me in the dressing room, said hi to me at school on Monday. In the school yard after lunch, Ty Pulleyblank nodded to me and threw me a basketball. I dribbled it and thrust it up at the net. I don't know who was more surprised, me, or Ty, when it rolled around the hoop and dropped in through the mesh.

"Cool," he said. "Try one from back here." He was dribbling the ball about five metres out from the net. He punched it down hard so that it would go way up high, and I stepped in to catch it when it came down. I spanked it a couple of times, like I've seen on TV, and jumped it up high. It was headed for the net. It was a sure ringer. That's when Roddy Smith threw his basketball at it. The balls collided and went off in different directions. Ty went to get his ball from over by the swings, where the little kids were playing.

Before I had a chance to decide whether I should say something smart to Roddy, the bell rang, and I headed into class. We had history right after lunch, and Mr. Straight, our home room teacher, also taught history. If I had done my history homework that weekend, things might have been different. I had looked over the stuff on American space exploration, but I hadn't read it carefully.

Mr. Straight was very tough. I had already been in trouble with him once for not doing homework. I don't think he liked me. I figured that I could keep my head down and bluff my way through the class.

No such luck. The moment everyone was in the room, Mr. Straight started the class. "We'll be looking at the space race. I suppose you've all had a chance to read the chapter?" he asked. "Lester Lewchuck," he looked right at me, "who was the first man in space?"

"Me?" I asked.

"I don't see anybody else in here named Lewchuck." He looked around the room like he was checking for Lewchucks. "Have you had your ears cleaned lately?" Everybody laughed. Mr. Straight shrugged his shoulders and sort of smiled. "So. Who was the first man in space?"

I didn't even think about it. I just blurted out the first name that came into my head. "Buzz Aldrin?" I knew it was probably wrong, but I knew somebody named "Buzz" had gone to the moon.

"Are you reading the same book as the rest of us, or have you got a different textbook?" Now I was really embarrassed. Everybody was looking at me. I didn't have any idea who the first man in space was. He was waiting for me to continue. "Is that your final answer?"

I had read some of the chapter on space exploration, but I couldn't remember all the names. "What about Neil Armstrong?" I answered, hoping for a lucky guess.

"What about taking your book and sitting in the hall with it until you've read the chapter." I thought he was kidding, and I laughed and looked around at the other kids.

"Come on, Lewchuck, take your book, get out in the hall, and read it." He swung the door open and I just sat there with my mouth open. "Let's go, Lester. I expect my students to do their part. Come back when you've read the chapter."

"I *have* read the chapter." I stood my ground. "I can't remember the name of every guy who goes up in space. What about Alan Shepard?"

"Not even close, Lester. You've earned a detention. Out!"

I grabbed my book and slunk to the front of the room. Everybody was looking at me. I figured they thought I was stupid, so I guess I just had to prove it to them. "I'll get you for this," I muttered under my breath.

"What did you say, Lewchuck?" Mr. Straight yelled. By now the whole school knew I was in trouble. "You think you can expect to cruise through my class without doing any work? Make it *five* detentions or tell me what you said!"

"He said he'd get you for it!" Roddy Smith piped up. He sat there grinning, pushing his glasses back up over his nose.

"Well, you won't get me for it today, Mr. Lewchuck! I'll meet you at the principal's office. You can go *there* and read the chapter!"

So off I went to the office, where I spent the rest of the afternoon re-reading the chapter. The principal's secretary asked me if I was there to see Mrs. Chung-Robertson, the principal. "No ma'am," I said, "I'm just here to re-read my history book ..." She didn't say any more, and just smiled at me every time she went in or out of the room. People came and went and she answered all their questions. Every time someone came in, they looked at me like I was a criminal. I felt pretty stupid.

After school, Mickey came to find me in the office. I was still waiting for Mr. Straight to come down, but he never showed up. Mickey said she saw him leave the school and drive off, so we left the office and headed home.

Mickey lived on the next block and had to pass my place on her way home. "You want to get a shake at the East End?" she asked. The East End Diner is a place on Queen Street where you can get tasty food cheap. They specialize in milkshakes and greasy french fries with gravy. A lot of the kids from our school hang out there.

"I don't know. I think I should get home." I didn't have any good reason to go home, I just didn't feel like making my first appearance at the school's favorite hangout after spending the afternoon in the office.

"Come on, Les, I'll buy." That was all it took. If there is one thing I can't resist, it's a freebie.

We headed down to Queen Street and into the East End Diner. There was a bunch of kids in the restaurant. I had seen a lot of them at school, but I didn't know many of them. Mickey said hi to some kids and pulled up a chair at the table next to them.

"Hey, turkey, are you still lost in space?" It was Roddy Smith. He was sitting with his brother and Delgatto at the back of the restaurant. Delgatto was laughing. "Is the Spaceman out on a date with the Queen of the Cage?" Roddy continued.

"Ignore them," Mickey said, loud enough for everybody in the restaurant to hear. "They're not worth the time of day."

I did. I sat across from Mickey and she introduced me to her friends. "Les is new on the Metro Cats," she explained.

"Hey, Lester," Roddy called from the back of the restaurant. "Who's the first man in space?"

I ignored him.

"Have a nice time in the principal's office?" he laughed. "Loser Lewchuck here is *gonna get* Mr. Straight!" he explained to Lenny and Delgatto. He was explaining it to everybody in the restaurant. "He's so dumb he doesn't remember what he read last night!"

I'd had it. I probably should have just sat there and taken it, but I didn't. "Can't these lunks read?" I said, loud enough for them to hear me at the back table. "The special of the day is pork chops. It's probably their mom on the menu." Mickey started to laugh. Delgatto stopped laughing. Lenny stood up and he and Roddy slid out from their table. I knew I had gone too far, but I just couldn't stop myself. "If I were them, I'd curl up my little tail and get out before I found myself in the frying pan!"

"You're pushing your luck, Spaceman," Roddy yelled. "You're gonna be the *next* man on the moon." Delgatto and Lenny moved over to where we were sitting. I had a pretty good idea of what they had in mind, but I didn't think they were going to start a fight in the diner. Lenny picked up the menu from our table and waved it at me. I stood up, and Mickey stood up.

"OK. That's it!" The waitress broke it up. "You three hoodlums get out of here right now. We're not going to have any trouble here. You two," she pointed at us, "sit down and shut up. I don't want any trouble."

Lenny and Roddy let fly with a string of swear words and strolled out of the diner. Delgatto followed behind them, giggling to himself. "We'll see *you* later, Spaceman," Lenny yelled at me through the glass. "Watch your back, man."

"I've been thinking, Mickey," I said to her when the waitress came with our shakes and french fries. "I don't think I'm cut out for playing hockey. I think I'm going to wait for baseball season."

"So they got to you, eh?" she said, with a french fry between her teeth.

"No! I just don't want to play a stupid game with a bunch of thugs. I mean, it's OK for you, they don't hit on you like they do the rest of us. And Coach Coleman! You think I *like* to play for a smelly old codger with an attitude problem? Coleman, Smith, Delgatto — they're all goons. I don't know how you stand it!"

"Well, for one thing, we're a pretty good team. We're probably going to win the Eastern division. For another, I've spent a lot of time teaching you how to play. Besides, they may be jerks, but the Smiths are also pretty good players. And Delgatto's not so bad once you get to know him. You'll see. It's better when they're on your side. A lot of the other teams are afraid of us. Just try a couple of real games. It's OK. You'll like it."

I didn't have a good answer for her. I didn't want to look like a wimp, so I agreed to stay on the team. I didn't like the idea too much, but I liked Mickey, and Ty was a pretty good guy, and maybe if I got to be friends with some of the other players it would be better. It couldn't be worse.

So it was a pretty lousy Monday all around. The rest of the week wasn't much better. By the time Saturday morning arrived, I was ready to do some serious body checking in the Metro Cats season opener.

4

"Great Team You Got Here!"

Saturday was game day. My first game with the Metro Cats. My dad woke me up early and made me breakfast. His apartment has a tiny kitchen, but he still makes a great Saturday breakfast. Eggs, bacon, and home fries with onions and curry sauce. I didn't like the curry at first, but when you mix it in with the egg yolk, it's great.

It was a sunny morning, and it had snowed a lot the night before. We went out to the parking lot and dug out my dad's car. It was covered by a deep layer of light, sparkling snow.

My dad is a quiet guy. Most of the time he reads. He works for a company that sells books to libraries, and sometimes I think he reads every one of them before he sells them. He's always got his nose between the covers of a book about oriental carpets, or religion, or something or other. A lot of the time when he talks to me, I don't know what he's talking about. It doesn't stop him, though. He just goes on and I pretend to understand. Sometimes I think he's too smart for his own good. My mother says he's overeducated. She's probably right.

On the way to the rink, my dad said he couldn't stay at the arena, but he'd be back to catch some of the game. He had some things to take care of. I was disappointed that he wasn't going to be there for my first game, but at the same time, I was sort of glad he wouldn't be there in case I really blew it.

In the dressing room, I sat next to Ty and the two of us mumbled to each other and had a laugh about Coach Coleman. He came into the locker room and clapped his hands together. "Let's go, men, game time in fifteen minutes! Let's make it count today!" He checked some things off on his clip board and headed out of the locker room.

We didn't seem to be a team at all. Some of the guys knew each other, but mostly, we were fourteen kids who hadn't really learned how to play together. We couldn't even *talk* to each other. Then the Smiths came in. Lenny was smoking a cigarette. Roddy threw his bag down next to the bench and started pulling his shirt off. Delgatto came in a few minutes later and went straight to the bathroom. He came back and started pulling his gear out and hanging it up piece by piece, on the hooks behind his seat.

"Listen up, turkeys." Lenny stood up on the bench in the middle of the room and waved his cigarette around. "We're gonna *win* this game today, and I'm gonna tell you how we're gonna win it. If any of you get the puck, you give it to me or Delgatto. If you can't get it to one of us, you can give it to Roddy. Or even Miss Priss if you have to." Delgatto laughed at the Miss Priss part, but nobody else did. As I looked around the dressing room, almost everybody was busy looking at his skates, or adjusting equipment. Nobody was looking at anybody else. "Whatever you do, don't try anything stupid. None of you are any good, so just give the puck to somebody who can score with it. Roddy, who won the scoring title last year?"

Roddy looked up at Lenny and swore at him. Finally, he answered. "You did," he said.

"And who was second?" He was squishing the cigarette between his fingers and fiddling with it so it would go out. Finally, he just spit on it and threw it over by the toilets.

"Delgatto," Roddy chimed in the answer. Delgatto thought this was hilarious and nearly fell over laughing.

"And you turkeys," he waved his arm over the bunch of kids with their heads between their knees. "Who's gonna win it this year?"

Nobody said anything.

"I said, *'Who's gonna win it this year?'*" he sneered around the room, waving his arms, like he was conducting an orchestra. "Who's gonna win it this year?"

"Roddy!" Delgatto said. It was the first thing I had heard him say in two weeks. He had a high, squeaky voice, and he must have thought it sounded funny, because he laughed like a loon on a moonlit night.

"Just remember," Lenny said, stepping off the bench. "Give the puck to somebody who knows what to do with it. And no heroics!" He tucked his long hair into his helmet and yanked on his equipment.

We all clacked out onto the rink. I felt like a steer on the way to the slaughter house.

Once the puck was dropped, it was a free-for-all. Nobody could do any of the plays we were supposed to have learned at practice, but it didn't matter. Wherever the puck was, there was either a Smith or Delgatto to take it. It didn't matter what team the puck carrier was on, they'd knock the guy as hard as they could, and skate off with the puck. It was pretty weird to watch players knock down their own team mates.

Lenny dropped the puck to Roddy, and Roddy circled in the center ice zone, waiting for the team to regroup. Ty was in the clear at the Tornadoes' blueline, screaming for the puck. "Smith, over here! Smith! Gimme the puck!" Roddy was still circling, waiting for Lenny to get clear. "Smith, I'm clear!"

Everybody could see that the other team was swarming Lenny, and leaving Ty alone. Two Tornadoes players converged on Roddy, and the puck squirted free.

"It's about time," Ty screamed, as he picked up the loose puck. "Let's go!" He crossed the center line and waited for Lenny to catch him up at the blueline.

"Gimme the puck, Tubby!" Lenny called. Ty crossed the blueline with the puck on his stick.

"No way!" he shouted back. I guess he figured he waited so long to get it, he was going to keep it for a while.

Before Ty got two strides closer to the net, Roddy slid up behind him and grabbed him by the back of his pants. "See you later, Fatso!" he laughed, as he yanked Ty down onto the ice and cuffed him in the head with the back of his gloved hand. The puck skidded off into the corner, and the referee blew the whistle.

"Two minutes for roughing!" he called, pointing at Roddy.

"You can't give me two minutes for roughing *my own guy!*" Roddy hollered. He was really angry.

"I can give you anything I want, tough guy. You want to make it five for unsportsman-like conduct?" Roddy just dropped his head and skated for the penalty box. He was mumbling swear words just loud enough so we could hear him, but not loud enough to get himself in more trouble.

My first game as a Metro Cat was not shaping up the way I expected. It was bizarre. By the end of the first period, I had been on for three shifts and had never touched the puck. Delgatto had scored twice, and Lenny had scored once. And our team had had six penalties. A guy with long black hair scored two for the Tornadoes.

Early in the third period, Lenny Smith tripped the guy with long hair, and jabbed him with his stick. The referee gave him a penalty, and the coach sent Mickey out. She scored from the face-off, but the coach sent Lenny right back out when they let him out of the box. I couldn't believe it. Mickey was as good as he was, and she didn't get penalties, but she spent most of the period on the bench.

The only people having any fun were the coach, the Smiths, and Delgatto. The other team got a few laughs at the way our team played, like there were three teams on the ice instead of two. The referee was as disgusted as I was. He came over to the bench a few times and argued with Mr. Coleman. He kept telling him to control his players, especially "the big guy," Lenny. "Somebody's going to get hurt out here!" he warned.

"Don't worry, I'm keeping the girl right here on the bench where she won't get hurt. Now you do your job, and let me do mine!" Mr. Coleman was a real good sport.

When Glen Macklem, our best defenceman, was body checked by Lenny, he couldn't take it any more. He reached out his stick and pulled Lenny's skates out from under him. The ref blew the whistle, and Lenny started swinging at Macklem. He jammed Glen up against the boards and jabbed him with the blade of his stick.

"Are you crazy?" Lenny hollered. "Whose side are you on, anyway? I'm gonna win this game, you idiot! I told you woosies to pass the puck to *me!*"

"That's not the way I play, Smith. I don't go around knocking down *our players!* If we're going to win, we do it as a *team*. Who do you think you are, Wendel Clark?" Glen's face was pure red. His hair was sort of orange, but his face was bright as a McIntosh apple.

"Well, freak you, turkey!" Smith said, grabbing Glen by the shirt. He started pulling the jersey up over Glen's face.

"Yeah, and your mother," Macklem yelled back, pushing Lenny's hands away and jerking away from his grip. They both had their helmets and gloves off. Lenny was a lot bigger than Glen, but Glen was holding his own.

"OK. You two save this for the dressing room!" The referee skated in between the two of them and pulled them apart. "You," he pushed Lenny, "into the box. Two minutes for roughing! And you," he pointed at Macklem, "sit out your two in the timekeeper's area."

Glen skated over to where the timekeeper sits, flung himself over the boards, and slammed his stick down on the bench. Lenny took his time picking up his stuff before going into the regular penalty box, grinning the whole time.

"Great team you guys got here!" the Tornadoes player with the long hair said to me. "We don't have to beat you, we just have to skate around and let you beat yourselves!"

With two men off for two minutes, the Tornadoes easily tied the game on the power play.

The referee could see that it would be pretty stupid to put Lenny and Glen together in the penalty box. Somebody was bound to get hurt. Coach Coleman wasn't so thoughtful. When the Tornadoes scored, and the penalties were canceled, Coleman put Lenny and Macklem both on the bench, right next to each other. It was one of the meanest things I've ever seen. Lenny kept calling Macklem a lot of things you can't find in the dictionary, and jabbing him with the butt end of his stick.

When the Tornadoes scored the go ahead goal near the end of the period, Coleman leaned over to Macklem and put his hand on his shoulder. He spoke just loud enough for everybody on the bench to hear him. "Nice going, kid. Proud of yourself, are ya?"

I couldn't stand it any more. I took off my helmet and walked to the dressing room. There was still five minutes to go, but I didn't care. I didn't care who was going to win, and I didn't care to play any more. Maybe it was important enough to Macklem, or Ty, or Mickey, but I wasn't interested.

I was dressed and out front of the arena waiting for my dad before the game ended.

My dad didn't make it to the game at all. Finally, I saw his Honda come around the corner. I threw my stuff into the back seat and mumbled at him. "You didn't make it, eh," I said.

"No, sorry," he said. "I was visiting a friend at the hospital."

"That guy from your office?"

"Yeah. He's sick. He's not going to make it."

"You mean … "

"He's got a sort of cancer … Well, not cancer. He's dying."

I wanted to tell him about the game. About the coach, and the Smiths. But I could see he wasn't in any mood to talk about hockey. I didn't want to bother him with my problems so I kept it inside, and he drove me home in silence.

When my mom and dad separated, they told me that I still had *two* parents, only they weren't going to live together. It was starting to feel like we all had separate lives, like he had his life, and I had mine. I missed not having my family.

When my dad stopped the car in front of my house, I hugged him, and he drove off. I watched his Honda stop at the stop sign, and wished that we could have talked about the man in the hospital.

I unlocked the front door and dumped my bag under the coat rack. I heard somebody in the basement. The person was whistling. I knew it wasn't my mother; it was a man. At first I thought I should call out 'hello!', then I thought I should get out. Somebody was in the house. Maybe somebody dangerous?

I opened the door quietly and slipped out on the porch, pulling the door behind me. I figured that I should go next door and ask to phone. If nobody answered, I'd call the police.

Then I saw the note on the door:

LESTER:
   MR. JOHNSON WORKING IN THE BASE-
   MENT. HOME AT DINNER, YOUR TURN TO
   COOK.

                                    LOVE, MOM

Mr. Johnson was a cool old guy. He hardly ever said anything, but he'd been a friend of my grandfather, and I'd known him since I was a baby. "Hello!" I called out, heading back in and down the stairs.

"Hello, Les," Mr. Johnson smiled up from his sawing. He could fix anything, this guy. I don't think I ever saw him at our house when he wasn't either building something, fixing something, or explaining to my dad how to do something. He was that sort of guy.

Tom Johnson was pretty big. He stood well over six feet and had a grey brush cut. The most distinctive thing about him was his hands: they were huge and soft looking.

"What are you building?" I asked. He had some sawhorses set up and a pile of lumber was neatly stacked along the wall.

"Oh, your mother wanted some closets put in down here, and some book cases for the living room." Mr. Johnson had a shop just down the street from the arena. He was usually working in his shop when I'd go by, and he'd wave at me. "You been playing hockey?"

"I'm not sure. Maybe I've been to a dogfight. It was hard to tell the difference. Whatever it was, it was the last time I'll do it."

"Gee, son," he frowned. "That's too bad. I guess you lost, eh?"

"Lost?" I laughed an angry laugh. "I don't know. I don't care. I left before it was over. Hockey is a game for thugs." I don't remember what I said next. I just ranted and raved about the stupid coach and the juvenile delinquents who get all the goals and glory. Mr. Johnson just stood and listened.

"Have you got any coffee, son? I'd sure like a cup about now." His expression was strange, like he was really mad.

We went up into the kitchen and he put some cold coffee in the microwave. "Lester," he said, "you're going to find them everywhere. Bully boys. And I can't tell you what to do about it. You can't let 'em spoil your life, though." The microwave beeped and he took out the cup and stirred it quietly for a few minutes. "You know, son, I don't talk about this much, but I'm going to tell you something." He leaned back into his chair and got comfortable.

"Did you know that I played hockey?" he asked, his blue eyes burning in on me.

I shook my head. I didn't really know anything about Tom Johnson, except that he and my grandfather were friends, and that he had a shop on Coldwell Avenue.

"I played for the Toronto Maple Leafs, you know."

He had to be kidding. He could see that I doubted what he was saying. "You can look it up. The record book says 'Tommy Johnson' and I'm him.

"And bullies, I'll tell you that I worked for one of the worst bullies of all time. I was on the front line of Major Conn Smythe's Army. I saw a lot of bully boys in my day. But I never let them stop me. I couldn't beat them, and I couldn't bring myself to join them, but I learned how to let them *slide* off my back. Some of them made the headlines every night, but I just went about playin' my game. I didn't get headlines, but I did a good job."

"You can have a lot of fun playing hockey. You call it a thug's game. It doesn't have to be like that. You see these guys on television playin' some newfangled game that looks a bit like hockey ... *that's not hockey*. They call it the NHL! Ha! You want to see hockey, you go watch the kids play in the park. Watch the ones who aren't so good, but who try hard. *That's* hockey, not all this grabbing and jabbing for millions of dollars."

"You don't like hockey either, eh?" I asked.

"Like it?" He laughed a sort of angry laugh. "I loved the game. I played every day of my life when I was young, and I loved it.

"But the guys who run professional hockey are like the guys who run everything else, and they take all the fun out of it. After nearly fifteen seasons my heart wasn't in it any more. And I was past my peak. I didn't need hockey, and it didn't need me, I guess. I wasn't in it for the glory ... I was in it because I loved the Maple Leafs. Blue and white blood ran through my veins. So when they traded me, I packed it in. That was it. No more hockey. To me, the Toronto Maple Leafs were like, like my life. My family. I was proud to be a part of the team. I gave them everything I had in me.

"But the guys who ran the game didn't think like that. To them, I was just a player. After fifteen years of service they traded me for some farm hand in the Detroit organization. That hurt me more than any of the bad hits I'd taken in Chicago or Detroit. It hit me where it counts. So I hung up the skates." He put both of his huge, pink hands down on the table in front of him and pressed the thumbs together.

"And I've never played since. I can't watch it, I don't like to hear the scores on the radio, and I don't like to talk about it. You know," he laughed a hurt sort of laugh, "every month, I get a small pension cheque from the NHL Players Association, and I mark it 'return to sender.' They keep sending them, and I keep sending them back. We been doin' it for years ...

"I can't tell you what to do, Lester. But if you let them beat you, you might live to regret it …" He had finished his coffee, but he kept trying to sip the last drop. Finally, he set the cup down and got up. He seemed a lot taller than he had before. Maybe you expect a hockey player to be bigger than a guy who fixes things. I don't know. "I'm on my way, son, but don't make any quick decisions. Talk to your friends about it. Maybe they all feel the same way. Maybe they'd all like to do something about it. I don't know."

Mr. Johnson went down to get his toolbox, and I took my hockey bag up to my room. He said good-bye and closed the door behind him. I stayed in the kitchen and got out a bag of potatoes and started peeling them for dinner.

My life as a jock was not going well, and I had a feeling it was going to get worse before it got better.

5

"Go Get 'Em, Tiger!"

I thought a lot about what Mr. Johnson had said. I figured that anybody who had played for the Toronto Maple Leafs was worth listening to. But really, he hadn't said that much. Maybe he regretted never playing again. He seemed to understand about the Smiths, and the coach, and it made him mad. Maybe the bullies he knew in hockey were like the Smiths, getting all the goals and all the glory. But he said that he still loved the game, and that it could still be a lot of fun.

That's true. I always had a good time playing with my friends in my old neighborhood. We argued a lot, but it was OK. We would divide up the available players, and somebody would always call the plays, yelling like Joe Bowen: "Lewchuck fumbles with the puck in the corner … He gets away from Peacock … He crosses the blueline … *Pass* across to Feldman, … *Feldman* whips the puck at Rosso, he shoots! Rosso dives … He scores! Feldman, at 4:04 in overtime! Feldman *scores!*"

It was fun. Not like with the Smiths.

Mickey telephoned Sunday morning. I was still in bed, and my mom called me to the phone. "So what happened to you?" Mickey asked.

"You mean after the game?" I said.

"Well, no, I mean in the third period. When the coach called for the shift change, you weren't there. He was yelling all over the arena. Ty did a double shift, and he got an assist on the winning goal." She sounded really mad.

"I suppose Lenny scored it, right?"

"No, it was Roddy. What's the matter with you?"

"What's the *matter* with me? You mean you *like* playing with those morons? I couldn't stand it any more. Between the coach, the Smiths, and the referee, I thought it was a three-ring circus. Why don't they let you play goal? And why do the Smiths get twice as many shifts as everybody else? And how come the coach lets them get away with shoving everybody around?" I hadn't decided to let her have it, I just couldn't help it.

"Because they're good! They're probably the best three players in our division, and we've got a chance to win the championship. That is, if our defencemen don't go home because they're mad every time they see a play they don't like!" She was yelling into the phone now. "Are you going to be there today?" We had a game at two o'clock that afternoon.

"I don't know," I said flatly.

"You don't know? That's the way you think the game works? You come to the games when you want to? Well, it's not, Les. You're either *in* or you're *out!* So I'll see you." And she hung up the phone.

I thought about what Mickey had said. Maybe she was right. The Smiths were rough players, and they were creeps, but they *were* good players. We won the game after all. And they weren't the only ones acting stupid. I decided to give it another try. I didn't want to be a quitter. I decided to go to the game and give it a shot. Maybe it would be different.

My dad called and asked if he could come to the game. He sounded sort of excited about going. Maybe he felt guilty about missing yesterday's game. My mom said she was going to do some Christmas shopping anyway, so it worked out for everybody.

On the way to the game, my dad stopped outside the hockey store across the street from the rink. With all the games at the arena on Sundays, they stayed open all weekend. He said that since I was playing, I should have a new stick. We went to the back of the store and I started leaning on first this stick, and then the next. My dad was looking over the skates and stuff. Then I heard a familiar high-pitched squeal at the back of the store. It was Delgatto's laugh.

I could see the back of Delgatto's jacket in the aisle. He was talking to the guy who worked in the store, asking him questions. Then I saw Roddy at the front of the store. He was fidgeting with his glasses, and looking back at Delgatto every few seconds. He picked up a helmet and put it down again and then started looking over the team jerseys. He was watching Delgatto from the corner of his eye and looking over his shoulder. Then he picked up a book from the counter and pretended to read a few pages, then quickly slipped it under his jacket. I was just about to yell at him, but I froze and watched Roddy casually stroll out of the store. I couldn't do anything. I should have told my dad, or called the store manager but I just stood there gawking

Delgatto left a few minutes later. We took the stick to the front of the store, and my dad talked to the guy, who was now at the cash register. I picked up the book from the small pile on the counter. They were all the same book. It was called *Manon: Making Hockey History*. It was written by the girl from Quebec, Manon Rheaume, who played goalie for the Tampa Bay Lightning. I'd heard of her. I wondered why Roddy wanted that book.

My dad paid for the stick and we left. I guess I shouldn't have been surprised that Roddy would steal something, but I was. I almost admired his nerve. He was so smooth, like there was nothing to it. He lifted the book up, flipped through it, and slipped it inside his jacket.

"Did you see those guys in the store, Dad?" I asked as we crossed the street.

"Yeah," he said.

"Well, they're on my team … " I was going to tell him about the book, but I decided to keep it to myself. I should have told the guy in the store, and now I felt sort of stupid. "Never mind. Thanks for the stick. It's great."

I didn't tell him anything. Not about the book, or about Roddy. I didn't tell him about the game, and I didn't tell him about Mr. Johnson. My dad isn't a very good listener, and I guess I'm not a real good talker.

I was pretty nervous that he was going to stay for the game. My dad and I have played catch sometimes, and he takes me camping most summers, but we don't really do very much together. I'd rather he *imagined* the game than actually *saw* it. The idea of him watching me play kind of gave me the jitters.

He carried my new stick to the dressing room door for me, and ruffled my hair. "Go get 'em, tiger," he said. I wish he hadn't said that. The dressing room was full of guys, and they all heard it.

"Hey, Tiger," Lenny said, as soon as my dad was safely out of earshot. "Are you gonna hang around for the whole game this time, or are you going to suck out when the going gets tough?" He turned to Delgatto and pointed at me with his thumb. "He's not a tiger, he's a pussy cat."

"Why don't you drop dead." It wasn't the smartest reply, but it was all I could think of.

"You know for a suck, you sure talk big, Lewchuck. I'd like to see you use your fists as well as you use your mouth.

You're gonna pay for all this you know. Everybody pays sooner or later," Lenny scowled at me.

"Tell it to your kid brother, the kleptomaniac," I mumbled.

"Wha'd'ya mean by *that,* Loser?" Roddy yelled at me. He probably would have come right over and belted me if he hadn't been tying up his skates.

"Nothing, only something reminded me of where I've seen you before. You're Cro-Magnon man, aren't you?" I said. I've always believed that the best defence against guys like Roddy is to confuse them. He probably would have punched me out right then, skates or no skates, if he knew what a kleptomaniac was, or that Cro-Magnon man is a big, ugly human ancestor, but he never got the chance.

I was saved by Coach Coleman, who came into the dressing room right on cue. I was near the door, so when he came in, I was the closest person to him. He smelled like whiskey. "A'right, men, game time in five. I expect you to get out there and play like Metro Cats, not like a pack of pussy cats! We got lucky yesterday."

Mr. Coleman turned around and saw me lacing up my skates. I kept my head down, watching what I was doing.

"What happened to *you* yesterday? You know a hockey game has *three* periods. You're expected to stay for the whole game!"

I shrugged, but I didn't look up.

"What we've got here is a hockey team, sonny boy. I'm the coach, and you're a player. *I'm* in charge. *I* say when it's time to go, not you." He looked down his nose at me and folded his arms. "If everybody around here just did what he wanted, what kind of a team would that be? Eh?" He didn't wait for an answer. "If you've got someplace to go after a game, you just make sure you go *after* the game. Not on *my* time. Is that understood?"

He looked at me, expecting me to say something, but I just continued tying up my skates, playing dumb. I could see that he was shaking his head at me. "Keep your head up, Lewchuck. We don't like quitters around here. And put a little padding in your seat, you're gonna see a lot of bench time today ..."

6

A Little Respect

The coach was as good as his word. The Metro Cats made mincemeat out of the Beaches Bulldogs while I sat on the bench for the whole first period.

The Bulldogs had one really good player, and she was on defence. She scored once, and set up a couple of close shots, but Roddy scored one from center ice and Ty slipped one in from the side of the net when everybody was digging for the puck. My dad was sitting a few rows up in the stands, on the other side of the ice. He was talking to Mr. Johnson.

Mr. Johnson kept pointing at the players and my dad was nodding. I felt pretty stupid sitting on the bench when my dad and Mr. Johnson had come to see me play. I didn't want to say anything to Mr. Coleman, because I knew he would tell me to buzz off. I just bit my lip and waited it out.

When we went to the dressing room between periods, everybody was pumped up. We were ahead by a goal, and it didn't look like the Bulldogs had what it would take to beat us. Mickey came to the dressing room door and knocked.

"OK if I come in?" she asked. "Everybody decent?"

"Anybody want a *girl* in here?" Lenny asked.

"Sure," Roddy spoke up. "Come on in! I've even bought her a little present."

Mickey waddled in and sat down on the bench. Coach Coleman was in the bathroom. We could hear him coughing and grunting, and Delgatto sat on the bench imitating him. "Think he'll be out in time for the face-off?" Mickey laughed.

"Like it matters?" Roddy answered. He pulled the book about Manon Rheaume out of his bag and tossed it to her. "Here. This'll give you something to shoot for!"

"Wow. Manon Rheaume! She's my idol!" Mickey flipped the book over and looked at the back of the jacket.

"Yeah," Ty said. "I've heard about her. She plays for the Tampa Bay farm club. Too bad she'll never make it."

"Oh, yeah?" She threw the book at Ty. "Why not?"

You could see that Ty couldn't give a right answer. "Mickey, she's a girl! No girl is ever going to play in the NHL! Sure she played in an NHL *exhibition* game, but the chances of a girl making the big club in the NHL are about zero. They're not strong enough."

"Yeah, well you remember that next time you're clear and I've got the puck, eh?" Mickey grinned.

"Yeah, OK, I get the point, Mickey," Ty shrugged, "Maybe she *can* make it, but it's a long shot."

"I've got a better shot at it than *you* do, and you remember that when you're in the corners," she laughed.

Delgatto was pealing with laughter. He slammed his hand up against the lockers and banged his helmeted head. Everybody was laughing now. It felt like we were a team for the first time since I joined.

The coach was in the bathroom. We could hear him yelling at us to wait until he told us we could leave the locker room. Lenny rolled his eyes and pointed his thumb in the direction of the bathroom stalls. "Get him," he chuckled.

"Let's move. Two minutes till the whistle." We trooped out to the bench, still laughing and joking.

I looked over to where my dad and Mr. Johnson were sitting. Glen Macklem, the kid who got the penalty for tripping Lenny Smith in the last game, was sitting with them. Another man was sitting there, too. I figured that the man had to be Macklem's father, since he had the same pointy face and red hair. I couldn't hear what they were saying, but I could see that Mr. Johnson looked mad.

When Mr. Coleman came out to the bench he was steaming. His face was purple, and I swear I could see his ears wiggling. He started yelling at Lenny, telling him that he expected him to act like a captain, not the coach. "When I say you stay in the locker room, you keep these jackasses in the locker room, do you understand, Mr. Scoring Champion?" Lenny was smiling like he didn't care, and Delgatto was still laughing. "You and your monkey here are on the bench. Miss Canada, center ice. You take the face-off. Pulleyblank, left wing; and you, " he pointed to me, "you're on the right wing! Don't screw up."

Maybe he forgot that Ty and I were defencemen. Maybe he forgot about Roddy. I don't know, but I looked at Mickey and Ty. They were both grinning from ear to ear. So was I. He sent two more kids out to play defence, and we skated to our positions.

The ref called Mickey and the Bulldogs center for the face-off, and Mickey won the draw. She flipped the puck over to Ty, and I made a break for the blueline. Ty passed the puck to me, and I got my stick on it. I crossed the line and saw both of the Bulldogs defencemen closing in on me. I should have shot it into the corner, but all I could think of was the goal. I didn't think about the fact that two defencemen coming at me meant that either Mickey or Ty would be open, I just shot the puck between the Beaches defencemen. It was right on target, but the goalie easily knocked it into the corner. Mickey picked it up and skated in behind the net. She started to move to the left, and both defencemen went after her, rounding the net on the left side. She quickly spun around and passed the puck to me. I snagged it and looked for a way to get it past the goalie. He had me covered. I could hear Ty calling me from behind somewhere, and I slipped the puck between my feet, and right on to his stick. He wound up and let it go. The goalie dropped to his knees and swiped at the puck, but he had no chance. The puck sailed past his glove hand and dented the mesh. It was four to two!

We slapped each other, hugged and laughed like crazy. The guys on the bench were all standing up cheering for us. Ty was skating around Wayne Gretzky style, with one leg bent at the knee and his stick waving in the air. My dad was on his feet, giving me the thumbs up. It was great! *This* was a team! *This* was what hockey was about.

I skated back to my position, and Mickey lined up for the face-off at center ice. The Bulldogs left winger stood right next to me. "Nice pass, man. How come you didn't play the first period?" he asked.

"Ask the coach. I dunno." I said.

"Your coach is drunk, isn't he?" he laughed.

I hadn't thought about it. Coleman smelled like liquor, but I had never thought about whether he was drunk. "I dunno," I said. The referee was busy talking to the captain of the Bulldogs team, and we all sort of shuffled around, trying to get a bit closer to the face-off.

"*Our* coach says he is. Maybe that's why he forgot to play you guys last period," he laughed.

Mickey won the face-off again, and as if by magic she had the puck on my stick. I dropped it back to our defenceman, and tried to get clear of the guy who had been talking to me. He was shadowing me. I was getting a little respect.

Our defence was great. Rick passed across to Sid Diamond, and Diamond slapped it right back to him, splitting the forward players perfectly. Rick waited for Mickey to come around to center ice and slid the puck up ice for her. She gathered up the pass and broke for the blueline. I was right behind her. She crossed the line and slipped the puck across to Ty. Ty was clear, but only for a second; two Bulldogs were barreling in on him.

Ty was perfect. He was the biggest kid on the ice, by about ten kilograms. The two puny kids racing in on him were at full stride. He scooted the puck behind his skates, stuck out his butt, and waited for the crash. The whole arena erupted with laughter and whistles. Ty stepped over the two sprawling Beach Bulldogs and pulled the puck back onto his stick. I came huffing and puffing across the blueline, making a beeline for the net. The downed defencemen were on their feet and all over Ty. "Les," he yelped, "go for the net! Go for the net!"

I took his pass and wound up for the shot. The goalie set up to block it. "No!" said a voice from behind me. "Hit me, Lewchuck!" It was Mickey. She was flying past me, right for the net. I poked the puck right on to her stick, and she swept it into the goal in one smooth move. The whole arena jumped to their feet. There were only about thirty people in the place, but it sounded like the Montreal Forum in Stanley Cup overtime. Mickey, Ty and I were hugging each other, and the defencemen were jumping all over us.

We skated to the bench, and the coach sat all three of us down. The Smiths and Delgatto took our places on the ice. It was OK, we were tired. We were on top of the world. But we were on the bench. When the shift change came, the coach sent out three more kids, and let them stay out for about two minutes. Then he sent the Smiths and Delgatto back out. We were still on the bench. Every time there was a stop in play, the three of us jumped up, waiting to be told to go over the boards.

The call never came. There were thirteen kids on the team, and the coach only played eleven of them. We kept getting up, waiting to be told to go out, but he never called us into the game. I was getting madder by the minute. I turned to Mickey. "What is going on here? We were *amazing!* Why isn't he letting us play?"

"He's the coach," Mickey answered quietly. I could see she was really mad too, but she just kept her eyes on the puck, and said, "You don't ask, you just do what he says. First rule of the game. He's the coach, you're the player. That's how it works. We can gripe about it later, but right now, you just do what you're told."

I couldn't believe it. Here she was, probably the best player on the team, maybe the best goalie in the league, sitting here on the bench, carrying a forward's stick. She should've been in the net, keeping pucks out, not riding the bench. And while she was sitting there, watching from the sidelines, the Bulldogs had scored three goals and tied the game.

When the team went to the dressing room between the second and third periods, I stayed on the bench. After a few minutes, Mr. Johnson came down and went into the visitors' dressing room. He didn't look too happy.

Our team came out to the bench looking like a bunch of losers. Nobody was smiling, and nobody was saying much. "Roddy, Center; Lewchuck, right wing; Delgatto, left wing." We jumped over the boards and skated into position. Roddy lost the draw. The puck skipped to my side. I got enough of my stick on it to shove it over toward Roddy. He skated into the defenceman and lost it. Our goalie stopped a shot and passed the puck out to Delgatto. The Bulldogs swarmed him, and he passed to Roddy. I was clear, Roddy wasn't. The Bulldogs centerman intercepted the pass and skated it to the slot. He shot wide of the net. Mike Malone picked it up in the corner and passed it out to Roddy. Roddy skated it into the center zone and lost it before he got to the blueline. Every time I was clear, the pass went to Roddy or Delgatto. I was yelling like a banshee the whole shift, but nobody ever passed me the puck.

After two shifts with this line, I wasn't thinking about the game any more. I was just thinking about getting my stick on the puck. I kept yelling at Delgatto, and Roddy, and Mike Malone, but they never passed to me. Roddy took a pass at our blueline and turned around to skate away with it. There was a defenceman between him and me, and I was clear all the way to the goalie. "Gimme the puck!" I shouted. "Smith! I'm clear. *Hello,* airhead, over here!" He passed to Delgatto, and I circled around to the other side of the ice. I was still in the clear; since everybody knew that the only time I ever got the puck was when I took it from somebody, nobody covered me. So they had extra men to get Delgatto. Delgatto passed it back to Roddy when they swarmed him. I started my useless calls for the puck, and looked around the ice to see who was where. "I'll bet you ten dollars that I can score if you give me the puck, Cave Man!" I shouted.

"Not for a hundred, Lewserchuck," Roddy sneered.

I don't know what got into me. It was probably the stupidest thing I've ever done. But I wasn't thinking about whether it was stupid or not, I just did it. I charged in behind Roddy, slammed into his butt with my shoulder, and sent him flying across the ice. I spun around once or twice, but I stayed on my feet.

I saw the Bulldogs defenceman sliding in toward the puck, and I slammed at it. I didn't look where the puck was going, but I got all of it. My stick came down and slapped it cleanly, with a fantastic *fwap.*

If I were a better hockey player, Roddy might have been seriously hurt. Since I've never been much of a shooter, the puck that I shot at Roddy Smith's rear end didn't do any real damage. He had trouble sitting down for the next couple of days, and Lenny told everybody about the bruise on his kid brother's butt, but only his pride was really hurt.

We lost the game, but Roddy and I both watched it from the bench. I sat on one end, and he sat, rather uncomfortably, on the other, swearing at me. For once I had a good time playing with the Metro Cats, but I knew it wouldn't last.

7

Roddy Rotten and
Lenny the Lunk

The dressing room was a circus. Nobody seemed to mind that I had knocked Roddy over and whacked him with the puck. Both Smiths were quiet, but Delgatto was laughing and making jokes about Roddy's butt with some of the other guys. "And all this time, I thought Lewchuck was a loser!" Delgatto shrieked. "His aim is perfect! Hit him right in the brains!"

Roddy was glaring at me across the room. "You're gonna pay for this, Loser," he said, over and over.

Ty spit on the locker room floor and sneered back at Roddy. "What are you gonna do, make him buy you a new bum? I guess your old one is cracked!" It wasn't like Ty to take a chance on getting involved. He usually kept out of it when the Smiths were getting to somebody. All of a sudden I liked Ty a whole lot more than I had before.

"I'll get you too, Pulleyblank." Roddy was almost crying. His face twisted up like he was about to burst into tears any second, but he managed to keep them from flowing. He wasn't used to having anybody make fun of *him*.

"Like maybe you're gonna get *all* of us?" Glen Macklem said from the locker room door. "Nice hit, Lewchuck. Next time, *you* knock him over, and *I'll* shoot him in the butt." Everyone broke up laughing, even Lenny.

Roddy couldn't stop himself any more. He got up and charged over toward me, fists flying, but before he got to me, three or four guys grabbed him and shoved him down on the bench. He was crying now, and all the kids groaned and whimpered along with him. Lenny grabbed up his kid brother and hustled him out into the hall. Delgatto packed up Roddy's clothes and stuffed them into his bag, and followed them out of the arena.

The whole team was laughing and giving high fives, like we'd just won the Stanley Cup. I was having a great time. All of a sudden, I was part of the team, and everybody liked me. Mickey stood outside the room and called in to us. "Is this a closed party or can I join in?"

"Yeah! Mickey," somebody yelled. "Come on in!"

"Anybody would think we *won* the way you guys are carrying on," she said. "We had this game in the bag."

"Yeah, Mickey, but it was *fun!*" I laughed.

"Oh, sure. Fun. So you knock down one of the best players and he gets hurt, and he spends the rest of the game on the bench, and we lose. Great." She was really mad. I didn't get it. Roddy had been asking for it. Even though I didn't *mean* to hit him with the puck, he was asking for it. And if everybody wanted to believe I gave him what he was asking for, well, what the heck?

"Come on, Mickey, he deserved it. If he'd have passed me the puck, I might have scored the go-ahead goal. He's a jerk," I said, sort of proud of myself.

"He's your centerman. When the timeclock starts, he's a centerman, and that's all he is. After the game, he's a jerk, or whatever you want, but when you're on the ice, he's your centerman. You don't knock him down and shoot the puck at him." She was serious. She was right, too.

But it didn't feel like that at the time. Here I was, enjoying having everybody on my side, and Roddy being babied out the door by his big brother, and Mickey starts lecturing me.

She was all dressed and ready to go, and I still had my skates on, so when she stomped out of the locker room, I just hung around with the guys and laughed about the game. Ty's dad was giving a lot of the boys a ride home, but I decided to walk. I had told my dad that I could make my own way home, figuring that I'd go to the East End Diner after the game. I thought I'd see Mickey there. So I packed up and headed out on my own.

I was feeling pretty good about the game. I knew I could play as well as most of the guys, and maybe now Roddy and Lenny would back off. Maybe Roddy would even pass me the puck next time. The snow crunched under my boots as I walked past Mr. Johnson's shop.

His shop doesn't look like anything from the outside. I mean, it doesn't look like a house, and it doesn't look like a store, either. He has a big front window, like a store, and curtains, like a house. It's weird. Inside, he has a collection of saws and lathes, and sanding machines, and samples of the stuff that he makes. There was a Christmas tree in the corner with its lights winking on and off, but I could see that nobody was there. The door had the 'closed' sign up and the curtains were half drawn. Mr. Johnson always kept them opened, and he worked where he could see the street.

"Hey, hotshot," I heard somebody call from behind me. Trouble. It was Roddy.

All of a sudden I didn't feel so good about being the guy who stood up to Roddy Smith. My stomach started churning, and I could hear my heart pumping in the sides of my head. I was scared to death.

"Hey, goof," Roddy called again. I wasn't going to stop, but I wasn't going to run, either. So I didn't say anything, I just kept walking. "I'm talking to you, goof!"

I could hear him puffing up behind me. I could smell Lenny's cigarette. There was nothing else I could do, he was right next to me, shoving me with his hand. I stopped.

"Where's your little girlfriend, hotshot?" he sneered. "All on your own, are you? If I were you, I'd have a body guard." He looked right at me, like he was a little crazy. "I mean a guy like you can have a lot of things happen to him. He can have accidents."

Maybe I should have told him that I didn't mean it. That I didn't hit him with the puck on purpose. But I didn't think he'd believe me, and I didn't want him to think I was afraid of him. "We're even, OK? Let's leave it at that," I said. I had my hockey stick in one hand, and my equipment bag slung over my other shoulder. I wouldn't have shaken hands anyway, but I couldn't even if I had wanted to.

"*Even?*" he laughed. "We're not even close, goof. You're gonna wish you'd never been born!" He shoved me with his hand, and I stumbled back a step or two. "Nice stick. A guy like you doesn't need a stick like that …" He shoved me again, but this time I didn't stumble. I bent my knees a little, and leaned into him.

"Just buzz off, Smith. I don't like you, and you don't like me. So what?" I said. "Why don't you go your way, and I'll go mine."

"You don't *get* it, do you? You don't just move in around here and think you can talk tough and act stupid. You're gonna *pay,* Lester Loser." He shoved me again, this time harder, and I stumbled backwards again. This time I ran into Lenny, who had snuck up behind me and knelt down, so when Roddy shoved me, I'd fall over him backwards. The old trick.

I guess it's an old trick because it always works. It worked perfectly. I went flopping around in the snow, my stick flying one way and my bag the other. Roddy grabbed my new stick and ran down the road. Lenny threw his cigarette butt at me and jogged up behind Roddy. "See ya 'round, sucker!" he shouted.

I was still sitting on the snow when I heard another familiar voice. "Trouble, Lester?" It was Mr. Johnson. He had just pulled up in his old pick-up in front of the store. The Smiths must have seen him coming.

"Trouble and how," I said, looking up and rubbing my elbow where it hit.

"Is that what they call hockey these days? I've seen some shenanigans on the rink, but I don't remember when I ever saw the likes of what I saw today." He had very thin skin on his face, and it always had a sort of pinkish look to it, but now it was beet red. "Have you kids ever had a *drill practice?* Have you *learned* anything about *the game?*" He looked really mad. He seemed to be completely different than I'd ever seen him before. It seemed to matter to him.

"I don't know," I said, grabbing his hand. He yanked me to my feet. "Maybe before I joined the team, I don't know. I doubt it."

Mr. Johnson pointed down the road with his thumb. "And those kids. Did they take your stick?"

"Yeah. I was kind of bushwhacked."

"Yeah, well, good talent gone to waste." He was squinting down the road, in the direction Roddy was headed. "A kid like that, with his reflexes, he could have been a good hockey player. But he's gone to seed already. Too big for his own britches. And gone rotten."

"You got that right. Rotten Roddy. And Lenny the Lunk." I felt like crying, but I was laughing. Mr. Johnson was laughing too.

"Come into the shop, Lester. I've got something I want to give you, and then I'll drive you home. We'll call your mother, and let her know where you are." I figured it was OK. I've been to Mr. Johnson's shop plenty of times.

I called my mom and told her I was there, and I'd be home in a while. She told me to ask Mr. Johnson to come for dinner. While I was on the phone, Mr. Johnson was in the back room, making a huge racket shoving furniture around. My mother wanted to know how the game went, so I told her it was fine and left it at that. I wasn't about to put her into her protective mother routine. She kept me on the phone for about five minutes. Meanwhile, I was looking at all the stuff Mr. Johnson had made.

Mostly, he had different shapes and sizes of moldings. He had samples that looked like picture frames, only they were big, for use around the edges of a ceiling, or on fancy furniture. It was amazing that anybody could actually *make* something like that. I thought all that stuff came from factories somewhere.

About the time my mother finished telling me something I can't remember, Mr. Johnson came out of the back room with a hockey stick.

"I wouldn't want you to go home without a stick, Lester." He stood an old, brown stick on its end and spun it around. "This here is a genuine piece of history. This is the last stick I ever used in a hockey game." He handed it over to me. "I made it myself." I looked at the stick, and then looked at him. He could see I doubted it. "I *always* made my own hockey sticks. I'm a woodsmith for heaven's sake!"

"It's not for a keepsake. It's to be played with. It won't break. And when it does, it should snap in the line of duty. So don't go hangin' it on a wall."

That's all he said about it. I tried to ask him questions, but he didn't want to give many answers. What I did get out of him was that the stick was made from ironwood which grows wild in the Don Valley, and that he played with a whole lot of players whose names I had heard before — Ted Kennedy, Max Bentley, Howie Meeker. I don't know who they are, but I've heard of them.

He had a fridge and a hot plate right in the shop. He put on a pot of hot chocolate and got cups from a cupboard. "You know, Lester, you can't let them get to you," he said, suddenly. "I understand why you shot the puck at that boy, but it's not part of the game …

"The great thing about a game, is that it's got rules. When you play by the rules, and you win," he paused for a minute, stirring his hot chocolate, "well, then you really won and there's no doubt about it … What did your coach have to say?"

"Not much. He yelled a lot." I didn't remember what he had said. I was thinking about what Mickey had said. It sounded a lot like what Mr. Johnson was saying.

"What you boys think of Mr. Coleman? He seemed to be a bit hard on some of you today …"

I was thinking about Mickey. "He's the coach," I said. "I mean, if he says sit on the bench, I guess you sit on the bench. I don't think he knows *anything* about hockey! I think he coaches because he likes ordering people around."

Mr. Johnson handed me a mug of hot chocolate. I took it and said, "Lenny is really the coach. He tells everybody what to do."

"I've seen guys like Lenny Smith before," he said. "I don't know what to do about them. They take over. They take all the fun and keep it to themselves. I've always just stayed out of their way myself. I'm not recommending that you slink away from them … I just let them know that I don't care much about them one way or the other. And I don't. I'm just sayin' that you can't beat 'em at their own game. You've gotta play *your game*. Use what you've got."

"All I've got is a big mouth," I said.

"Well," Mr. Johnson chuckled. "That's a start, I suppose ..."

"Yeah, well," I admitted, "I guess I did go overboard. I just can't stand it when Roddy tries to push everybody around. I don't want to be pushed around. If you just let him do it, then you've got the worst guy possible in charge. If you can make him look stupid, nobody will listen to him any more."

Mr. Johnson was nodding. "You've got a point there, Lester. A good point. I guess you should do what you think is best." He set his mug down on the counter top and looked hard at me. "And I've got to do what *I* think is best.

"Right now, I think it would be best if I got cleaned up and took you home. And then I think I'll make some phone calls."

8

Old Fogeys

My best friend was mad at me, I had the Smith brothers lurking around corners waiting to jump me and take my stuff, I had had detentions every night for a week, and I hadn't done any homework. I wasn't looking forward to school on Monday. I had a feeling I would have one of those stomach-aches that keep you home.

My mother knew something was up, even though I didn't let on. I don't think Mr. Johnson told her about what happened on the way home, but he must have said *something* because she was being extra nice and she wasn't bugging me about cleaning my room. Still, she wouldn't let me stay home.

I should have done my homework. I had time to get most of it done on Sunday night, but instead I sat on my bed with my books opened, doing nothing. I hardly glanced at the history stuff at all. So when I got to school, I was expecting the worst from Mr. Straight.

But Mr. Straight was away, and some lady who had lots to say about nothing filled in. Home room and history were a breeze. Roddy wasn't at school either. Everybody figured he didn't want to sit on his bruised pride all day, and we had a few laughs about him and his backside.

After school, I decided to knuckle down and do some homework. I got out my books and settled in to study. Then the phone rang. It was my dad. There was a practice at the rink at 5:30, and he was taking me for a burger on the way. What could I do? I put my books away and got out my hockey gear.

When my dad pulled up in front of the house, I grabbed my stick and bag, kissed my mom, and lugged my junk out to the car. My dad had the trunk open, and I handed him my stick.

"Where's your new stick?" he asked.

"I lent it to a friend," I lied. I should have told him that Roddy had stolen it, but I just swung the bag into the trunk and climbed into the front seat. I had to move his skates to sit down.

"How come there's a practice tonight?" I asked. "And how come *you* know about it and I don't?" I could tell from the look on his face that something was up.

"I had a call from Gord Macklem," he said. "Glen's father. The parents have rented the rink for a game of shinny. Apparently, they do it every Christmas. It's sort of a tradition. The Metro Cats against whatever team the parents can muster up. So, hey, I've got skates. I can play hockey. I'm not sure I was ever Phil Esposito, but I can carry the puck over the line."

I couldn't believe this was my father. *He* was going to play? First I was embarrassed. Then I started to laugh. I could just see all these old fogeys playing the Metro Cats. "You're kidding!" I snickered. "You guys against *us?*"

"Sure," my dad growled at me from behind the steering wheel. "Laugh all you like, but keep your head up in the corners!"

Everybody else was just as shocked as I was. The dressing room was wild. Everybody was laughing about their parents bringing their skates and sticks. We only had nine players.

Our regular goalie, Rollie Janise, didn't make it, so Mickey got to play in the net.

There was no sign of Mr. Coleman. Glen Macklem's father coached the Metro Cats, and the parents sort of coached themselves. They were pretty disorganized. From the beginning, the Metro Cats had control.

Syd Diamond won the face-off, and everybody groaned because his father was the referee, and he skipped the puck across to Ty. Ty turned with the puck and saw somebody's mother closing in on him. He bounced the puck into the boards, wove around her, and picked up the ricocheting puck heading across the blueline. It was Ty and the goalie. He wound up for a slapshot, and quickly deked to the side and slipped a wrist shot past the sprawled-out dad between the pipes. We erupted, giving high fives and whooping it up.

Syd came to the bench and I went out for the face-off. My opponent was a very determined mother with pursed lips. She had no intention of letting me get the puck. Her stare alone was enough to tell me that she was going to win the draw. And she did.

But once she had the puck, she didn't know what to do with it. It scooted off into our zone, and she was way too slow to get it. Glen Macklem picked it up and passed it across the ice. I skated for the blueline and made sure I got clear. *Bang.* Ty hit me with a forward pass, and I crossed the line. There were only three people in the zone: me, the goalie, and the defenceman. My dad.

He skated backwards, sweeping his stick low across the ice, trying to poke the puck away from me. I cradled it close, and cut hard for the slot. He was with me, skating backwards faster than I could ever have imagined. But he was screening me. I could see the goalie stretching to see me. He was trying to look over my father's shoulder.

"I can't see him! You're screening him! I can't see him!" the goalie bellowed.

I blew the puck between my father's skates and the cage plumber never saw it. A black blur pulled the twine and the puck sprung back out half way to the blueline. My dad grinned at me and shook his head, skating in a circle, bent over, with his hands on his knees.

With only eight skaters available, we all got a lot of ice time. Glen's father was a pretty good coach, mixing us up from defence to forward. We scored two more goals in the first period, and Mickey turned away every shot they got on her. We laughed and slapped each other all the way to the dressing room. Mr. Macklem gave us all high fives at the locker room door, and then he headed over to the other dressing room to console the parents.

We heard Delgatto first. He was laughing at something funny in the hall. Lenny was the first to come through the door. "How's it goin', turkeys?" he said. "The 'A' Team has arrived." Roddy and Delgatto elbowed each other in the doorway, laughing and poking at each other's bellies. Roddy had my stick.

I could either ignore it, or I could tell him to give me my stick back. If I ignored it, I wouldn't get the stick, and worse, he would have won. I figured my dad didn't buy the stick for Roddy. And I wasn't going to play it his way. "Nice stick, Roddy," I said. "Looks just like the one you took from me yesterday. If you ask me real nice, I might lend it to you for the second period."

"What?" He looked up, innocently. "This stick? My old Louisville Slugger? Naw, this is my stick, right Delgatto?" He poked Delgatto with the blade of the stick. Delgatto jumped away, shrugging.

"Lenny, this is my old Louisville Slugger, ain't it?" Lenny was tying his skates, laughing.

"Got your name on it, little brother?" he asked.

"Yeah, it does. It says right here. 'Slugger.' That's me!" Roddy grinned. He waved the stick toward me, showing me where it said 'Slugger.' He was just daring me to take it from him.

"*You* know it's my stick, and *I* know it's my stick. Everybody in the place knows it's my stick. And you think you can rip off my stick and nobody will do anything. Like nobody did anything when you stole the Manon Rheaume book, or when you show up late for practice. I don't know about anybody else, but I don't much like playing on a team with a thief." I couldn't stop myself. Everybody was staring at me. "So don't ask me if you can borrow my stick for the game." Roddy stood there with his mouth open. I looked at the stick. "The answer is no." And I took it easily out of his hands. He just stood there, like he didn't know whether to slug me or slink away.

"Game time!" Mr. Macklem burst into the locker room. "C'mon, guys, two minutes!" He turned to Roddy and Delgatto. "Great. Fresh troops." He nodded to Delgatto. "We can use you guys out there! I've been in the enemy camp. They think they're gonna come back this period!" he laughed, jerking his thumb in the direction of the visitors' dressing room.

"Yeah, like in their dreams!" somebody hooted.

Mr. Macklem herded us out to the rink, and Roddy came up with a stick from somewhere. Mr. Macklem tapped Lenny on the shoulder. "You're Lenny Smith, right?"

"In the flesh," Lenny beamed.

"Take center. Roddy, right wing." He turned to Delgatto. "And you take left wing."

"Left wing? Sure. Left wing. OK." Delgatto seemed to think left wing was very funny, but he bounced over the boards and glided smoothly across the ice to the far side, spinning in tight little circles.

Mr. Macklem watched the three of them shift and glide at center ice and he sort of smiled. "We'll give the fresh horses the first shift. Glen, defence. Ty, you partner him."

The referee dropped the puck, and the game was on. They scored a goal in about three minutes, but the line of Smith, Smith and Delgatto didn't ever play together again. Mr. Macklem was mixing us up, putting forwards on defence and defencemen on the wings, so that nobody ever played on the same line with the same guys twice.

And the parents were taking no prisoners. They whipped the puck from side to side and used their size to get through our lines. But it was no use. They could muscle their way across the blueline, but they couldn't beat Mickey Tanaka.

She was in her glory, shouting orders out of the net, telling us to clear the zone, or to get out of her sightlines, or yelling at us to let us know who was clear. Having Mickey in the net was like having eyes in the back of your head. She could see everything.

We won, of course. The Metro Cats 6, the parents zip. Everybody scored goals. Lenny scored one, Delgatto scored one, Ty scored two, Syd Diamond scored one, and I scored one. Roddy didn't score. He just glared at me all night.

I didn't care. I just played my game. I even passed him the puck a couple of times. I got my stick back. I had my say. And there wasn't a darned thing he could do about it. He sat across from me in the dressing room, joking and laughing as if everything was great, and then he'd stare at me for a few seconds. Behind his glasses, his eyes looked large and bulging. I stared back until he looked away. There was nothing he could do.

Mr. Macklem came in grinning. "You ought to see the *other guys!* You never saw such a pack of sore losers! They ought to travel with a team chiropractor."

Roddy grabbed up his stuff and left. Mr. Macklem slapped him on the shoulder on the way out. "Good game, Mr. Smith," he said.

Roddy sort of grunted something and walked to the door. He looked straight at me and pointed his finger, making a gun out of his finger and thumb. He fired at me and walked out of the room. Lenny and Delgatto weren't far behind him.

The rest of us were packed up long before our parents came moaning and groaning out of the dressing room. This time it was *us* waiting in the lobby, telling *them* to hurry up. We decided that it was only fair that the parents take the team out for pizza, and they went for it. A table for eighteen at the Tiny Emperor.

I have to admit that I never once thought about Mr. Straight or modern history class. One slice of pizza with the works was followed by another, and I never gave a thought to space exploration. For that matter I never gave a thought to Roddy Smith, or anything else that usually seemed so important. I just ate pizza, guzzled pop, and felt like a winner.

9

The Worst Day of My Life

On Tuesday morning, Mr. Straight was back. "Lewchuck," he said, as soon as the announcements were over. "You've had a week, *and* an unfortunate extra day. Have you read the next chapter in your book?"

"Yes, sir." I said. I hadn't exactly read it, but I'd looked at it at least.

"Good. Let's try again," he said, sitting down at his desk. "What was the purpose of the Gemini space missions?"

I tried to remember which was Gemini and which was Apollo. I stood up next to my desk and looked for the answer on the blackboard. No such luck. "To try to stay in space as long as possible."

"Oh, so you didn't waste your time in the office, eh? Great ..." I was still standing. He was going to grill me about the weekend assignment. "What was the purpose of the Apollo missions?"

"Ah." I knew this was going to be a disaster. "Which one?"

"The one in chapter six, Lester. The one you read about over the weekend. Remember?"

"Oh, yeah, it was to begin building a space station."

"A space station. You read the chapter?" He didn't wait for an answer. "Did anybody else read about building a space station, or is that part only in Lester's book?" Everybody laughed.

"Maybe you'd like to go back to the principal's office and read chapter six, Lewchuck. Chapter six. The one about the *moon explorations,* not the space shuttle. And you have another detention tonight." I packed up my books with a lot of banging and shuffling, and I stomped out of the room.

"Have a good time, Spaceman," Roddy whispered as I walked past him.

"Come on back and join us when you've read the chapter, Lewchuck, and we'll see how well you understand the moon exploration program." Mr. Straight closed the door behind me, and I made my way down the hall to sit in the office waiting room, and read my textbook.

People streamed in and out of the office, and everybody looked me over when they came in. The principal, Mrs. Chung-Robertson, asked me what I wanted. I told her that I was reading my homework from the weekend. She was a tiny, birdlike woman with a round face and a quick smile. She had her glasses down over her nose, and she looked at me over top of them. "Hmm," she said. "I understood that you were a pretty good student at Churchill Junior. You're not slipping, I hope."

"No, ma'am, I'm just not having a very good week," I said. She was cool. She just went into her office and closed the door.

A few minutes later, Roddy came by the office. He stuck his head in the door, and I looked up when he cleared his throat. "Mr. Straight wants to see you in the gym, Spaceman," he said. Then he disappeared.

I marked my place in my book, and headed off down the hall to the basement stairs. There was nobody in the gym. I went into the gymnasium office, and he wasn't there either, so I went back to the administration office. Mrs. Chung-Robertson was just coming out of her office when I came back in. She smiled at me and kept going. I opened up my book, and started reading again. I figured that if Mr. Straight wanted me, he knew where to find me.

About five minutes later, I could hear a high-pitched beep from somewhere. I stood up and went to the office door. Mrs. Chung-Robertson was running down the hall toward the stairs, and before she got there, the fire bell started to ring. The secretary told me not to leave yet, and then she grabbed a bunch of papers and a red binder from her desk. "Let's go, Mr. Lewchuck. This is no fire drill!"

I followed her out the door, and we joined the fast moving line of kids streaming down the hall and out the front doors of the school into the cold, winter air. Before all the kids had finished coming out, we could hear the fire trucks blaring up the road. They were there in less than two minutes. I wasn't sure whether I was supposed to stay with the secretary, or if I should go down to the end of the school where my class was lined up.

The secretary was too busy checking things off in her red binder to pay much attention to me. I stood by myself watching all the grade five and six kids shivering and throwing snowballs at each other. When the fire trucks arrived, Mrs. Chung-Robertson spoke to one of the firemen, while a whole lot of the other firefighters ran into the school carrying fire extinguishers.

We were all getting pretty cold. The bell stopped ringing after a few minutes, and the firemen started trickling out of the school and standing around the trucks. One of the teachers was gathering up slips of paper from the other teachers, and she brought them all to the secretary. I was throwing snowballs at the school, trying to hit the silver letters up on the second storey, over the doors.

The teacher who had been gathering up all the attendance slips called over to Mrs. Chung-Robertson. "We're missing one from Mr. Straight's class. Lester Lewchuck." I turned around when I heard her say my name.

"He was in the office. Isn't he with his class?" Mrs. Chung-Robertson asked, a bit panicky.

"I'm right here," I said, from right behind her.

"Why aren't you with your class? Don't you know you're supposed to report to your teacher?" She was pretty upset. "We'll talk about this later. Go let Mr. Straight know you're here."

"Yes, ma'am," I said. Great. Now I was in more trouble. Mrs. Chung-Robertson went into the school with the fireman she had been talking to, and the secretary stood at the doors, telling everybody that it was all right to go back in. I guessed it was a false alarm.

Mr. Straight gave me the hairy eyeball when I joined the class in the lineup to re-enter the school. I wondered what *his* problem was. Maybe he wanted me to go back to the office instead of the classroom. I don't know. Maybe he just doesn't like me.

We were in the class for about half an hour before the phone rang at the front of the room. Mr. Straight answered and looked over at me. "Sure. He'll be right there," he said. He looked over at me and called me to the front of the room. "Mrs. Chung-Robertson wants to see you. On the double."

What now? I wondered, strolling down the hall toward the principal's office. I guessed I was in trouble for not lining up with my class during the fire. Her office door was opened, and it was bulging with people. There were two firemen in all their equipment, a man in a black uniform, a policeman and a policewoman. I wondered what they would want with me.

The secretary asked me to sit on the bench by the door and wait. I could hear what the were saying in the principal's office, but I couldn't see the people from where I sat. "Yes ma'am, there's no question about it, it was arson. We found this stuffed in behind the door." I couldn't see what he was showing her.

"Well, I still can't believe it. I can't believe one of our students would put the whole school at risk …" Mrs. Chung-Robertson said.

"We'd like to have a talk with him just the same." The policewoman was doing the talking and her partner was writing things down in a small notepad.

"Let me have a talk with him first. What reason would he have to do something like that? I can't believe it." I didn't know who they were talking about, but I had a feeling it might be me. Naw, I thought to myself. They must be talking about somebody else.

Mrs. Chung-Robertson came out of the office and smiled at me. "Lester, would you come into the nurse's office with me?" Wrong again. They *were* talking about me. She was smiling, but I could tell she wasn't happy.

She didn't sit at the desk in the nurse's office, she sat on one of the chairs, and motioned for me to sit on the other one. "Lester," she said, very seriously, "are you having any problems at home?" I wondered what she was getting at.

"No," I said, uncertainly.

"Are things going badly here at school?"

"No, not really," I answered honestly. Things weren't great, but this *was* school, after all. When were things ever great at school?

"Lester, I have to ask you this question, I'm afraid. Now, I want you to think carefully and tell me the truth. It is very important that you tell me the truth. Do you understand?" She wasn't mad at me. It was more like she was sad. "Did you set a fire in the boys' washroom this morning?"

"Set a fire! No! I've been in the office all morning!"

"Well, Lester, that's not exactly true. You were in the office when I came in, but when I came out of my office, you weren't there. You had been out in the hall." She crooked her head to one side, like she wanted to believe me, but was disappointed that I hadn't told her the truth. Actually, I had forgotten that I had left the office.

"Well, yes, ma'am, I went to the gym. Mr. Straight wanted to see me there," I told her.

"Oh, good. Did you see Mr. Straight there?"

"Well, no, he wasn't there when I got there. I looked in the gym, and I looked in the office, and in the locker room. He wasn't there. So I came back here, to the administration office, and that's when the fire bell started, so I never even found out what he wanted." I had a feeling I was getting in deeper.

"What made you think he wanted to see you in the gym? Do you have gym class on Tuesday morning?" She knew the answer. We didn't *have* gym at all on Tuesdays. "Well, Roddy told me that Mr. Straight wanted to see me there."

"Lester, it is *very* important that you tell me the truth. A lot of people will be asking you questions, and you *must* tell the truth. This isn't a small matter. This is a very serious situation. There has been a fire set in our school, and the fire chief and the police have to find out how it happened. They will want to talk to you. Is that all right?" She seemed to believe me. She should have believed me, because I was telling the truth, but I knew a lot of people would think I was lying.

"I have called your mother, and the secretary is calling your father right now. Do you think we should wait for them to get here?" She was on my side. I could tell.

"I don't know … I don't have anything to hide," I said. I thought that was the right thing to say. I *didn't* have anything to hide, and I figured that if I offered to tell my story right away, it would be better for me.

"Just the same, Lester, I think we'll wait for your parents before we let the police talk to you. You know, Lester, I *do* want to believe you. I do not want to believe that one of my students would endanger the lives of the whole school. The consequences would be very serious. This is a very serious crime." She stood up and opened the door. "I want you to wait here, Lester, and don't talk to anyone unless I am with you. As long as you tell the truth, everything will be fine. Don't worry." Then she left, closing the door behind her.

10

Bad News

If you have ever sat in an empty room waiting for bad news, you know what it was like for me. My mother was at work, and she didn't show up for quite a while. In fact, the lunch period was over when the door finally opened and my mother came rushing in, a look of shock on her face, and tears gathering in her eyes. "Don't worry," she said. "Your dad is on his way. He'll be here in a few minutes. Why didn't you tell me you were having problems at school?"

"I'm *not* having problems at school! At least I *wasn't* until about two hours ago!" I wasn't going to cry, but I sure felt like it. My mom stood next to me and pulled my face into her belly. I felt a bit like a baby, but it also felt pretty good. At least I wasn't all alone any more. After a few minutes of telling my mother not to worry, the door opened, and Mrs. Chung-Robertson came in again.

"Your father is here, Lester. He's talking with the officers now. He'll be in here in a few minutes." She put her hand on my mother's shoulder. "If you'd like to go in with them, Mrs. Lewchuck, I'll stay with Lester."

"Should I?" My mother wasn't sure *what* to do. She'd never had a criminal for a son before. She looked at Mrs.

Chung-Robertson. "I guess I should. Les, will you be all right?" Now she was crying.

"Sure. I'm OK." It was starting to sink in that this was more serious than I thought. "Tell Dad I'm OK, Mom. I didn't do it," I said as she went out the door.

She stopped and turned around and wiped her eyes with her fingers. "I know, Les. I know what you are capable of, and I know you wouldn't do something like this." She believed me. I knew she would, but it was good to hear anyway.

"Lester," Mrs. Chung-Robertson said, "I've called the superintendent of schools. He's a very nice man, and he has a lot of experience with these sorts of things. If you just tell him exactly what happened, I don't think there will be anything to worry about." She was saying it, but something told me she didn't believe it. Something told me I was in more trouble than anybody was letting on.

She asked me what happened in class last week, and I told her about the whole thing. I told her about feeling like I was being picked on by Mr. Straight, and even though I hadn't read the chapter for today, I *had* read the stuff for last Monday, and I just couldn't remember who the first darned man in space was. She seemed to understand about being picked on, and she kept asking me how I felt about Mr. Straight. "Did you want to get him back for sending you to the office?" she asked.

"No. I was just mad that I was being sent out of class for nothing. I just couldn't *remember* who the first man in space was! I wasn't going to set fire to the school or anything! Is that what everybody thinks? That I set a fire to get even with Mr. Straight?" I couldn't believe it. I knew it was a stupid thing to say, but I didn't expect anybody to take it seriously.

Before she got a chance to ask any more questions, my mom and dad came in. They both looked worried. I wondered if I should be more worried than I already was.

"Hi, son," my dad said. "We've got our work cut out for us, here." He was dressed for work, wearing a jacket and tie. His thick glasses made him look very smart. Right now, I thought I needed somebody smart in my corner. My dad was the next best thing to a lawyer.

"I'll leave you alone for a few minutes. Let me know when you are ready to get together, OK?" Mrs. Chung-Robertson said quietly. She slipped out into the hallway.

"What did you tell them?" my dad asked. I told him exactly what happened, and exactly what I told Mrs. Chung-Robertson. He believed me. I could tell without having to hear him say it.

"Now, we're going to meet with a few people, Les. I don't want you to be scared. Just tell them what you told me. If they don't believe you, we'll fight it. Everybody *wants* to believe you. They just have to know what happened. They need to know that you didn't set the fire and then they have to find out who did.

"Setting a fire is a very serious offence. Setting one in a school puts hundreds of lives at risk, and they need to find out who did it. That's why they will seem so serious. It's heavy business. Don't be afraid, and whatever you do, don't be creative. Just tell them exactly what happened. Don't add anything, and don't leave anything out." I finally lost it. My eyes were burning, and the tears came up to put the fire out.

My dad continued getting me ready for my meeting with the police. "I know you had nothing to do with any of this, but think about it this way: You might know something that will help them figure out who did it. If you don't tell them every-thing you know, or if you make anything up, you will be helping whoever did set the fire. You're helping solve a crime. You're not a criminal." He stood up and I stood up. He gave me a tight hug, and my mom joined in on it. It felt really strange to be hugging both of them together. That hadn't happened in a long, long time, and it felt really great, like when I was a little kid.

"OK. Think you're ready, Les?" my dad asked.

"Yeah. I guess so. Who's going to be there?" I thought about the television shows I'd seen. I didn't expect any bare lightbulbs or sleeves rolled up, but I wasn't too sure.

"It'll be OK, Les. We're with you. We're all in this together."

I looked at the clock when we got out into the hall. It was 2:30. School would be over in a little more than an hour. The kindergarten class had been taken to the gym so that the police could talk to me in there. When we came in, there were about eight people already there. Mrs. Chung-Robertson introduced everyone.

The man I saw in her office was there. The one in the black uniform. His name was Mr. Antonio. He had a very soft face and a handlebar mustache. He wasn't smiling, but he didn't look angry either. When he shook my hand he looked me straight in the eyes. I felt very strange. Like I was guilty. I hadn't done anything, but I felt like I had. For just a second, I wondered if I *had* set a fire in the washroom. Maybe I set it and then forgot the whole thing. The feeling lasted only for a second, but it scared me. If *I* could almost believe it, and *I knew I hadn't done it* then how could I expect *them* to believe me?

The policewoman was talking to the man who was introduced to me as Mr. Vickers, the superintendent. He was a small man with a slim face and a pointy gray beard and very blue eyes. He came over to me with his hand out. When *he* shook my hand, it was like he was saying, 'I'm on *your* side.'

He took over the meeting. "Lester," he said, when we were all seated in a circle, "we'd like you to tell us whatever you know that will help us find the person who set this fire. We need to find out who it was so that we can make sure they don't do it again, and so that we can help them. If you don't want to say anything at all, that's OK too. That would mean that we would have to continue to investigate, and the police may be forced to question you themselves. Is that all clear? You are here to help us, and we are here to help you.

"Would you like to tell us about what happened to you this morning?" he asked, finally.

It wasn't what I expected. It wasn't the third degree at all. I did want to tell them. I didn't have anything to hide. So, once again, I told everyone what had happened: how I had been sent to the office, how Roddy told me to go to the gym, how I had heard the fire alarm and gone outside with everyone else.

Mrs. Chung-Robertson nodded at everything I said, and my mom gripped my hand. Mr. Vickers leaned forward. "Do you mind if we ask you some questions, Lester? You don't have to answer any of them, but it would help us."

"OK." My dad was nodding to me, letting me know he agreed with me.

"Did you have your math notebook with you when you went to the office, Lester?"

I thought about it for a second. I knew I hadn't brought it. It was on my desk. "No. It's on my desk."

"No, it's not on your desk, Lester," Mr. Vickers said. "I have it here. It is very badly burned, but we have some of it. Now, try to remember when you last saw your math notebook."

I couldn't believe it. How could he have my math book? And how could it have been burned? My eyes were stinging and I was ready to start crying. "It *was* on my desk. When I left the classroom. All my notebooks were there. I had just unpacked my knapsack. It's black." I couldn't believe it. How could my notebook have been in the boys' washroom?

"Are you sure that Roddy told you that Mr. Straight wanted to see you in the gym?"

"Yes, I'm sure. I thought it was weird to meet him in the gym, since we don't have gym on Tuesdays, but he definitely told me the gym. And that's where I went. I didn't go *anywhere near* the boys' washroom. So I don't know how my book got there." My dad sat up in his chair and whispered something to Mrs. Chung-Robertson. She shook her head a little and put up her finger, as if to say, 'Wait.'

It was Mrs. Chung-Robertson who spoke next. "Lester, Roddy tells us that when he came to the office you weren't there. Mr. Straight has confirmed this. He sent Roddy to get you from the office, and when Roddy came back, he reported that you were not in the office at all. But he *did* say that he saw somebody going through the boys' washroom door."

"That's a lie!" I cried. "He saw me. He stuck his head in and called me Spaceman or something, and told me to go to the gym!"

Mr. Antonio, the fire chief with the mustache, looked over at me and tried to hold my eyes again. "Did you tell Mr. Straight that you would 'get him'?"

"Yes," I said. I knew this wasn't looking good for me. Now I felt really stupid for talking back to Straight. "But I didn't *mean* it. I wasn't going to *do* anything. He was just being really mean, and I didn't like it. I didn't set the fire! I don't know who did!" I was going to cry any minute. None of them believed me.

"I think we could take a break here," Mr. Vickers stepped in. "I think Lester has told us all he'd like to tell us right now. Mrs. Lewchuck, would you and Lester like to have a snack in the staff room? There is coffee made if anybody would like some." He got up and opened the door, and my mom, dad and I went to the staff room.

11

Xavier

When we were called back to the kindergarten room, Mr. Vickers looked very different. He wasn't smiling. His eyes looked dark and serious. I knew it was bad. "Lester, Mr. Lewchuck, Mrs. Lewchuck. I'm afraid the police have decided to charge Lester with arson. The board and I will do whatever we can to help them get to the bottom of this. Frankly, I believe Lester. I don't think he's capable of this. I think there is more to this than we know yet."

I couldn't believe it. I had told the truth, and now they were going to arrest me for something I didn't do. My dad had his arm around my shoulder. My mom was crying, and he put his other arm around her and pulled her in for a hug. Just for a minute, I forgot that we were not a family any more. I forgot why we were all together. It felt good. Then the policewoman spoke.

"Lester, we're not charging you formally, but you will have to come to the station with us and speak with the detectives. Your parents can come with you in the cruiser."

The cruiser! I'm going to have to go to jail in a police car, I thought. I guess anybody would have cried.

Mr. Vickers and Mrs. Chung-Robertson walked with us to the parking lot. School was just getting out. The school yard was full of kids, and everybody was watching. Mickey was standing by the road, and she gave me the thumbs up. Ty Pulleyblank and Glen Macklem said hi to me, but I just looked straight ahead. I wished I had a bag to put over my head, like they do on the news. I saw Roddy and Lenny and Delgatto down by the edge of the school yard. Roddy stood with his arms folded, and he was grinning at me. Delgatto shoved him. He was yelling at Roddy. For once, at least, he wasn't laughing.

As we drove off in the police car, I saw Delgatto running across the school yard toward the small crowd by the parking lot. The Smiths were heading down toward Queen Street.

When we got to the police station, there was a message for the policewoman who had brought us in. We were led into a hallway with a lot of chairs and very bright lights. The policeman with us offered us coffee or pop, but none of us was thirsty.

It was strange, being with my mom and dad at the same time. When we all lived together, I never thought it was too bad. It wasn't like they fought and argued a lot. I thought we were a good family. Then something happened, and they split up. Boom. Just like that. One day they got along fine, and the next day they were separated. And nobody ever told me why.

We sat there for about half an hour. It seemed like all night. I wondered what was going to happen to me. Would they fingerprint me? Put on handcuffs? I had visions of television cop shows.

The policewoman finally came out into the hall. My dad got up and my mom stayed with me. The woman asked us to come into an interview room, and we all sat around an empty table. "Do you know somebody called Xavier Delgatto?"

"Yes, ma'am." I was just going to keep answering questions and telling the truth. I figured it was the only chance I had.

"Well, then you can thank him for saving your bacon. When he saw us take you away, he went to the principal and told her what he knew. I don't think we need to keep you here any longer. I won't apologize for bringing you in, though. I was just doing my job. I had the wrong guy, and now we may have the right guy. I hope so."

"*YOU* hope so?" I nearly shouted. "How do you think *I* feel?"

12

"Welcome Back, Lester"

We took a taxi home from the police station. My dad went to pick up his car from the school, and then he came in and got my mother's keys and went to get her car. When he came back, he was covered with snow, and he had a pizza with him. My mom helped him dust off all the snow, and she brought the pizza into the living room. It was weird. It was like old times. My mom's half had mushrooms and onions, and my dad and I had the half with the works. First we ate our half, then we started in on her half. Just like we used to do.

"Quite a day," my mom said. "I had a feeling there was something going on yesterday." She took the empty pizza box into the kitchen, and my dad and I shrugged at each other. "Come clean, Les," she said when she came back in. "Did you *really* have a stomachache yesterday, or were you faking?"

"Faking," I said. There was no point lying. It felt like we were all equals right now, like we were three adults, not parents and a kid. "I was afraid Roddy was going to get me for what happened on Sunday." As soon as I said it, I regretted it. My mom didn't know I had hit Roddy with the puck or that he had stolen my stick.

"What happened on *Sunday?*" she asked, like she was expecting the other shoe to drop.

I felt like it was finally OK to let my parents in on some of my life. I told my mom all about what happened on Saturday and then Sunday. She was laughing when I got to the part about the puck in the backside.

My dad wasn't laughing. He was sitting with his arms folded and his eyebrows crinkled up together. "So this Smith kid has your new stick?" he asked.

"No, I got it back. And Mr. Johnson gave me one of his. It's cool. He made it himself ..." I told them about Mr. Johnson and how he had played with the Leafs.

"You know, I'm not sure I even *like* hockey," I said, when the room went quiet. "I have a good time when we're just hacking around, but when it's important, I'm not sure I like it. The best thing about the whole game was when I saw Roddy squirm away from the puck. I'm not sure it's worth it. And I'm not very good."

"I think I understand everything you said except the last part. I thought you were great!" my dad said. I rolled my eyes.

"No, I mean it. Since we're all being so honest here, I'll tell you. I wasn't so sure about all this hockey stuff. I wasn't keen about you playing at all, but since you wanted to do it, I thought I'd see how it went. In fact, I called Tommy Johnson about it." I didn't know that. I thought Mr. Johnson was at the game to see me play.

"I called Mr. Johnson because I knew he was a hockey man, but I'd never talked about the game with him until now. Man, did I get an earful. It was like opening a bottle of champagne! When he hung up his skates, he hung up his past with them. I don't think he's seen, heard, or talked about hockey in thirty-five years. But I'll tell you, he's got a few opinions about the game!"

My dad was really relaxed. My mom got a pot of tea brewing, and the three of us talked about Mr. Johnson, my grandfather, and everybody else we all knew. It was amazing. I told them about Mickey, and her brothers, and they listened. And I told them about school, and Mr. Straight. And they listened. We talked for hours, and I was beat. I had to go to school in the morning. I went off to bed and left them talking. I fell asleep listening to them laughing and chatting downstairs.

As soon as I woke up, I knew that Wednesday was going to be better than Tuesday. My mom had already gone to work. I needed food. I found leftover pizza, which is the perfect thing to go with Cheerios.

I read my homework over the Cheerios and pizza. I read it very carefully. I made notes. I looked up stuff in the index. I memorized the names. I was ready for him. If Mr. Straight wanted to play hardball, I'd hit one out of the park. It was getting late. If I ran, I could make it to school before the bell. I grabbed my stuff and headed out.

When I got to school, they were waiting for me. It seemed like a hundred kids were swarming around me like bees around honey. Everybody wanted to know what happened, and I said I wasn't sure, but I thought Roddy was in a lot of trouble. They all laughed.

"No kidding!" somebody said. "Roddy has been arrested! And Lenny is being sent to live with his grandmother out east!"

"You're kidding! What happened?" I asked.

Before I had time to find out any more, the bell rang and we all headed into the school. I got to my desk and unpacked as usual. I was cool.

"Mr. Lewchuck. Good morning … " Mr. Straight had started already. "Glad you could join us." He crossed to the door and closed it. Everybody was waiting to see what he was going to say. He made us wait it out while he silently took the attendance and filled out the sheet at his desk.

"Mr. Lewchuck. We've moved on to the next chapter, but for the record, could you tell us anything about the space explorations of the 1960s?"

"Is there anything in particular you would like me to tell you? Or should I just start at the beginning?" I stood next to my desk, and looked across at him. I wasn't going to let him make me look stupid.

"Maybe you should begin at the beginning, if you like."

I shuffled my feet and rhymed off the facts in my head, trying to get it all straight. Then I began my speech. "In the late 1950s the Soviet Union sent a dog into space, and that was really the start of the space race. The Americans sent two monkeys up in 1958, and the Russians sent up two more dogs, and they orbited the earth for a day and a half. Next, the Russians sent a man, Yuri Gagarin, into orbit. He was the first cosmonaut. That's Russian for astronaut …" I spoke for about five minutes. "In 1969, Apollo 11 left the earth with three men aboard. Hours later, the captain, Neil Armstrong, radioed back to earth from the surface of the moon. 'That's one small step for a man … One giant leap for mankind.'" I sat back down at my desk and put my hands together in front of me.

"Good answer." Mr. Straight was stunned. "Welcome back, Lester." He was standing up, smiling. He clapped his hands in applause and nodded to me. "Good answer." It was over. I won. We were even.

We had a game on Saturday. We were playing the Tornadoes again, the team Lenny and Roddy beat up the week before. I figured it was going to be a bumpy game. The game was at three, but we were told to be there at noon. I went to the arena on my own. I could have asked my dad to drive me, but I told him I'd take the bus. Instead of going to his place on Thursday and Friday, they decided that *he* would come and stay with *us* instead. That was cool. It was *weird,* but it was cool. They were talking a lot on the phone. A lot. I figured it was a good sign. My mom asked me how I felt about having my dad come for Christmas. It was definitely a good sign.

I got to the rink at 11:30. Some of the team were already there, but nobody seemed to know why we were supposed to arrive at noon. We were trying to figure it out when a short fat man with a mustache came in to the dressing room.

"I'm Tommy Gaston," he announced. "I'm the league secretary." Everybody shut up and stared.

"We had to jump through hoops you can't imagine, but we managed to get you boys two hours of practice ice before today's game. I can't believe we actually bamboozled the East Metro Figure Skating Club out of two hours, but your coach insisted on it."

Nobody had any idea what he was talking about. He looked around at our blank faces and frowned. "Mr. Coleman won't be your coach any more. He has been asked to resign. You will have a new coach. He has agreed to coach your team on the condition that he gets two hours of ice time with you before the first game. And so here we are."

He looked at his watch. "And so, here we are at 11:50 with two hours of ice time starting in ten minutes, and your coach isn't here." He looked like somebody had told him a bad joke. His chin wobbled into pools of wagging flesh, and he sort of grinned over top of it. We all started to put on our gear. We could take the hint. "And so," he said again, "here we are with ten minutes, a dozen kids and no coach ..."

The door to the locker room opened. It was Glen Macklem. We heard a sharp blast of a whistle come from out on the rink. Glen opened the door so we could see out. There, at center ice, stood a tall man in an old-style Toronto Maple

Leafs jacket, with his hands cupped around his mouth. "Seven minutes, and no lallygagging!" he called.

"Ahhh," the fat league man sighed. "Your new coach. Mr. Tommy Johnson."

We all looked at each other and scrambled into our equipment. "If he's half as good a hockey coach as he was a player, you boys are in for the ride of your lives."

I scrambled over the boards and skated around the outside of the rink. Mr. Johnson was at the side of the rink talking to the man from the league. I was stretching and flexing, and getting my rhythm, thinking how good it was to be playing with no Smiths. And no Delgatto.

I wondered what would happen to Delgatto. The policewoman said he saved my bacon. I figured maybe he was OK. But he wasn't here, so I didn't have to worry about it.

Mr. Johnson introduced himself and said he wanted us to just play a game of shinny for a few minutes so he could see how we skated. I was on a line with Mickey, and we were doing great. She fed me a pass and I skated up ice. Ty was out of position, so only Glen Macklem was between me and the goalie. I heard a call from my left. "Right behind you, Chucko!" It was Delgatto. He was just behind me and to my left. I crossed the blueline and dropped him the puck. Macklem went for Delgatto and I went for the slot. *Bang*. Delgatto hit my stick. The goalie was out for a hot dog on the other side of the net, looking for Delgatto to shoot, and boom! "He shoots, he scores!"

And so began my winter as a Metro Cat. It wasn't all goals and glory. It was a lot of hard work, and a lot of fun. Delgatto and Mickey and I played a lot together. We were a pretty good line. We made it to the playoffs and played a team from York in two nailbiters and one heartbreaker. None of us won any trophies, but when it came to the end of the season banquet, we were definitely the loudest table in the place!